THE SCARLETT JOSHUA'S FOLLY

Book II in The Sacred Blade of Profanity series

Toneye Eyenot

Edited by: J. Ellington Ashton Press Staff

Cover Art by: Michael Fisher

http://jellingtonashton.com/

Copyright.

Toneye Eyenot

©2016, Toneye Eyenot

ALL RIGHTS RESERVED. This book contains material protected under International and Federal Copyright Laws and Treaties. Any unauthorized reprint or use of this material is prohibited. No part of this book, including the cover and photos, may be reproduced or transmitted in any form or by any means, electronic or mechanical, including photocopying, recording, or by any information storage and retrieval system without express written permission from the author / publisher. All rights reserved.

Any resemblance to persons, places living or dead is purely coincidental. This is a work of fiction.

***DEDICATION**
This book is dedicated to my father, Thomas Francis
Donohoe, who left this world on the 18th of August 2014.
He was 88 years old.
Be at Peace, Dad xo*

Acknowledgements and Thanks

After the completion of **The Scarlett Curse**, *the love, support and encouragement of my family and many of my friends to continue has been inspirational. Catt Dahman, Susan Simone, Amanda M Lyons, Jim Goforth, David McGlumphy, and all of the family at J. Ellington Ashton Press; You have all taught me heaps and shown me much support, respect and kinship. You accept my strange ways (haha). Thank you all! Following the sound advice of Jim Goforth, eye found my Home in JEA, and am very glad eye did.*

To everyone out there who has read The Scarlett Curse, thank you all so much for your support, and eye hope you enjoy this prequel. It should shed a lot of light on book 1, while giving you some fresh circumstances to both; look forward to and dread. Hails 'n' Howls to all of you!

Special thanks *have to be made here, to the man in the shadows. The man who asked to be kept out of the spotlight with The Scarlett Curse. Credit, however, must be given where it's due. Tony Noel, my old and dear friend, you didn't say anything about this book, haha! You transformed me from a pen and paper, technophobic novice into a semi competent keyboard author. You've been like a mentor to me with your advice and help on these 2 books. This series would still be a pipedream if it weren't for you, so, sorry Brother. Eye couldn't not give you your fully deserved props! Thanks Legend! Cheers and Hails! ~Toneye*

Jahl-Rin… the very name would cause folk to look over their shoulder in terror. Not Joshua though. Joshua Melkerin was a peculiar character. Unassuming, ordinary looking, generously aged; he was not the kind of person one would consider to engage in the despicable acts such as those of Jahl-Rin and his ilk. His colourful past, a meticulously kept secret from all decent and law abiding folk, Joshua had at last reached the point of no repent. Alone in the world and the last of his ancestry, his zest for life all but extinguished, Joshua cared naught for the fortunes of others.

The Sacred Blade Of Profanity had waited many years to introduce itself, through Scarlett, to Joshua's tainted blood. The time had come at long and final last. The Kirlt'th sorcerers' lineage had their motivations behind each targeted kill throughout the extensive history of The Blade Of Power—motives that would one day become apparent, as Joshua plodded uncertainly to his inevitable doom…

CHAPTER 1

Jahl-Rin wiped the grease from his mouth, and spat the tiny shards of bone and stringy meat onto the table beside his plate.

"If I have to eat another godsdamned quail this week," he muttered under his breath, "I'm gonna eat that fucken fat prick of a cook." He downed his whiskey, pushed his plate across the table and stood up, all in one swift and agitated movement. His foreboding presence was felt throughout the inn at the sudden, imposing action.

A large meat knife attack to the front left of his skull that he had weathered from a long past bar room battle, had left Jahl-Rin with an impressive looking trophy that travelled in a gracefully serrated arc, along and down to the bridge of his wide, flattened nose. The subsequent nerve damage caused the left side of his face to drop slightly, and he was forever wiping drool that gathered in the pocket of his hanging lower lip. His fierce temper was matched by his skill with a sword or a stick, indeed, anything close by and handy he could pick up and use to quickly end a fight before it began. Woe would come to those who fed this terrible temper.

Jahl-Rin seemed to transform. He would seem larger… much larger. His skin would take on a darker hue, and though his voice dropped to a menacing, growling whisper, his rage-filled, blazing eyes, and spit hanging from his mouth, flicking this way and that—this would be the last thing you would see.

"Marnard! Where you hiding, boy?" Jahl-Rin cast

an inebriated eye around the crowded room. He and his men had arrived at the Sarls Bend Inn two nights previous. Within the hour, they pretty much had the run of the place. Two whole days and nights of debauched revelry that saw many of the local patrons quickly take their leave, lest they be subjected to the drunken torments of this bawdy, rowdy crew.

"Haha! Here he is, Boss!" Marnard felt two large hands clamp down painfully on his tired shoulders, before being dragged to his feet from behind some crates of wine. "C'mon boy. Whaddre ya doin' back there? Did ya lose ya balls? Aahahaha!" Cold pricks of spittle tickled the back of Marnard's neck, and the stench of gods-know-what emanating from this goliath's mouth, along with his slurred words, held the boy frozen in terror.

"The boss called you. Move!" And with that, the poor lad was sent bouncing and spinning from one drunken bandit to the next, to unintentionally fall on one knee at Jahl-Rin's feet.

"Get up, boy. Flattery will get you nowhere," Jahl-Rin sneered at Marnard. "And many thanks, my good man, for flushing out my little rat here," he added, roughly patting Marnard's greasy, matted locks as he stood up nervously.

"Most welcome, Boss," replied Jahl-Rin's old friend and right hand man, Goatus Of Torment, or 'Goat' in short. Leering cheekily, he offered his alpha a deep bow. A poorly masked gesture of mockery, which backfired on the heavily intoxicated giant. The bow transformed into a forward stumble, that culminated in a headlong pitch across a crowded table, to the uproarious laughter of his comrades.

* * *

Just beyond the limits of Sarls Bend, a small group quietly gathered. News of the bandits at the inn had reached

Seth Bellen, the town's self-appointed lawmaker. In reality, he was no less a common thug than Jahl-Rin and his unruly mob. Yet, as with Jahl-Rin, there was nobody in Sarls Bend with the intestinal fortitude to stand up to his tyrannical rule. Those who had tried in the past were either made a very public example of—or had simply and mysteriously vanished. He owed his position in Sarls Bend solely to his name and nothing more. The Bellen name spanned the four hundred years that had passed, as his ancestors had built the majority of Sarls Bend and effectively owned the town. Seth was the last of his line, and it was likely to end with him. A completely hateable man with not a single redeeming quality. There wasn't a woman by any stretch of the land who would tolerate Seth Bellen, let alone bear his spawn. The arrival of the well-known and well despised Jahl-Rin put the fear of every god into the coward, Seth Bellen. This however, manifested as a convincing masquerade of bravado, with the accompaniment of his seemingly loyal band of 'deputies' at his back.

It was indeed testament to the cowardice of Bellen that he would rally from the safety of outside Sarls Bend to plan a sneak attack. A bold and, by all accounts, foolish confrontation with the likes of Jahl-Rin and his mob was hardly a desirable plan of action to Seth. Surely, his ragtag posse also shared this sentiment, as the bully coward of Sarls Bend put forward his strategy.

"Nerrik, take your brother and find the barkeep. I understand he was run out of the inn early last night. Send him here and be quick about it."

Nerrik looked to his brother Joav, who had not been paying attention, and gave him a sharp elbow to his arm.

"Huh? Ow!"

"Just come with me, idiot. Let's go." Nerrik scowled at his halfwit brother, "I'll explain on the way."

"Uh-huh," shrugged Joav, and began to follow

Nerrik back down to the cobbled road that led into Sarls Bend.

"When you've done that, get over to my stables and wait for me there," Seth called out to Nerrik, who threw a casual salute to Seth and a clip 'round the ear of Joav, as the two brothers strode off towards the road. The remaining seven men and three women stood by, anticipating their orders.

* * *

Across the Bay of Solace, along which spread the fishing village of Terrinus, and some hundred and seventy miles northwest, beyond the vast expanse of Mellowood Forest, the sorceress Astra Kirltth sat in deep meditation. Her humble abode - a cave which lay well hidden from prying eyes amidst a rocky outcrop, served her needs perfectly. From her position, she could view clear across the Sunflight Ranges, west to the ancient city of Eve.

Astra's needs were very few, actually. A place to sleep, prepare her food and most importantly, to practice her craft. All else was secondary in priority and importance in her day-to-day existence.

An uneasiness was brewing in the realm of void. An ancient foresight of what was to come reached through the veil to this world, and took up an unwelcome residence in Astra's very bones. It was becoming increasingly difficult for her to focus her attention and energy to where it had long been assigned—The Sacred Blade Of Profanity and its wearying host, Scarlett.

The Watcher, as the title would suggest, could perform that task and nothing more. Only watch…Witness. It was the responsibility and burden of Astra Kirltth to tap into, interpret and act, according to what the Watcher beheld.

The Watcher had been a man once. More than eight

thousand years into the illusive past, he had been a sorcerer of enviable wisdom and Power. Part of an ageless order of seers and intimately involved in the crafting of The Sacred Blade Of Profanity. He had walked this earth plane for more than five hundred years. An inconceivable impossibility for the average mind to comprehend, yet, as with the fellow sorcerers of his lineage, a common occurrence, regardless.

The discovery of void, so many millennia past, by these archaic seekers of knowledge, sparked a fervent delving into this realm of infinite possibilities. This carried through the ages, as their Power and thirst for knowledge grew substantially and evermore precipitously, leading to the realisation that the more time they spent exploring void, the less human they were becoming—the less physically distinguishable. Their energy bodies began to transform. The egg-like shape began to stretch. As this progressed, they found their scope of perception greatly increase, as it allowed a much larger volume of the energy, or awareness of void to pass through their being.

The peril of this exercise in Power was evident, as the more time they spent in void, the less chance there was to retain human form. They knew, or *saw* that there was definitely a point of no return…but what wonders must lay beyond that point? The Watcher, whose human name had since become a long absent utterance on the tongues of men and itself become void, volunteered graciously and perhaps somewhat greedily, to be the necessary link between the sorcerers of old and the other realm. Over centuries, the energy body of the Watcher stretched to a line that endeavoured towards infinity and gradually but surely lost not only the ability to return, but also to effect change in the world of form. An exorbitant price to pay that the Watcher, and indeed the entire order, had been deviously kept unaware of. Void, after all, is pure awareness and moulder of perception, which necessitates the awareness of other beings in order to continue in its infinite expansion.

With a deep and controlled inhalation, Astra collected and shifted the emphasis of unease that pervaded her being, to the symbols patterned in the dirt before her crossed legs. She kept her breath momentarily as she peered at the strange and ancient symbols, which began to swirl and interchange. A sharp, loud 'PAH' exhalation exploded the now transformed sigil into a vision of The Sacred Blade. Around its frame, letters began to form in an arc, revealing to Astra and in turn, to The Sacred Blade Of Profanity itself, a name…

"Joshua Melkerin. Finally!" His time on this earth was at hand, to which end, The Blade showed great elation and excitement

CHAPTER 2

A disturbed Scarlett awoke, drenched in sweat and feeling short of breath. A clandestine urgency brought her into a sitting position as she struggled to wake fully.

"*We have work to do, Scarlett!*" The voice snapped her out of her post-slumber listlessness, and she felt the pulsing energy of The Blade Of Power in its sheath. The name, '*Joshua Melkerin*' played behind her weary eyes.

"It does ring a bell," Scarlett groaned aloud to The Blade. It seemed to have been tapping impatiently on the side of her ribs as she lay with it inside her loose fitting sleeping shirt, which had facilitated Scarlett's abrupt, yet well-rehearsed awakening. As she sat in lotus on her bed, Scarlett relaxed her eyes and allowed them to remain closed. Internally shaking off those final remnants of sleep, her mind became incredibly clear.

"*Joshua, yes, I know who that is.*" Scarlett turned her speech inward to engage conversation where both were most at ease and more intimately linked. "*He runs three businesses in the town of Mills Wall. He's very influential, and also very private and secretive. He is one not to be trusted."*

The town butcher, a tailor store, and a small but very successful shop that dealt in odds and ends were owned by Joshua. From extravagant rarities to everyday conveniences, ranging in fee to cater for all, be it pauper or prince. Not to mention his farming expertise. His own garden grounds were the envy of vegetable and fruit sellers for many miles and from numerous towns and villages, who continuously passed through Joshua's grounds to purchase stock for their respective businesses.

"Oh Scarlett, that is such a transparent picture you have conjured up of Joshua Melkerin. There is so much more to him than meets the eye. Even your keen eye, Scarlett. He is a scoundrel, and I have waited some years to make my 'personal acquaintance' with him."

Mills Wall was more than half a day's walk from Scarlett's hut. Hidden in some of the deepest and thickest of Mellowood, Scarlett resided frugally though resiliently. A consummate hunter, she seldom went hungry. It would be two hundred and ninety years by next moon since Scarlett had become interconnected with The Sacred Blade Of Profanity. In those centuries she subsisted, and along with the many advantages afforded Scarlett by The Blade Of Power, she had grown supernaturally expert in many things. The tiny hut, barely accessible from the trees, was built by Scarlett's own hand. No one else knew of its existence; discounting the forest fauna and two especially large ravens, who had flown through the open door, landing themselves noisily on the table at which Scarlett had just sat for the first time in her new abode. They skipped their way around the large, flat table, seemingly oblivious to Scarlett as they flapped their wings intermittently and investigated their surroundings. Their gaze passed by her, just out of unison, without stopping or acknowledging her, then they hopped their way back to the beginning point of arrival, and flew straight back out the door.

The next day and every day thus, the ravens returned. Only then, they would greet Scarlett directly and immediately on arrival, sometimes carrying gifts of forest berries in their beaks, which they would drop on the table and then caw softly, staring straight at Scarlett until she'd move to pick them up. They would jump around the berries at her approach, and hop quickly along the table, just before she scooped the berries up in her surprisingly soft hands; their little game of 'raven tag'. The Sacred Blade Of Profanity and its immunity to the constraints of Time and Space had left Scarlett physically identical, bar a few battle scars, to the moment she had first wrapped her hand around this tragic weapon of immeasurable Power. Twenty? Twenty five? Scarlett couldn't remember her age from that long ago. She only knew she had followed her path now for nearly three centuries.

* * *

Joshua had been awake for hours—since the wee hours, when he woke suddenly from probably the best slumber of his life and just couldn't get back to sleep. He had been struck with the certainty that he was being watched at that very moment. In the blinding darkness, Joshua had feared someone was in the room with him. Now he was tending to his vegetables and various fruit trees, in an attempt to quiet his racing mind and calm his nerves. It was as if he didn't have enough on his plate, that he was filled with trepidation at meeting with Jahl-Rin. Apparently, he had a deal to strike that would make Joshua a lot more well off than he currently was. Every encounter with the bandit traders, however, was a terribly unnerving one. Jahl-Rin could switch in the blink of an eye, from an accommodating albeit intimidating host, to an insane, homicidal demonstration of unfounded fury. Luckily, Joshua had never borne the brunt of his wrath; yet for those who had, one would be at a loss to figure out the whys and wherefores surrounding Jahl-Rin's chosen target.

He now couldn't shake the feeling that he was being watched. Not just watched. Analysed... judged. He felt there was nowhere to take refuge from this probing ethereal eye, as it followed him wherever he would be, though Joshua could not detect the source. The source was unknown. It was hidden—Occult.

* * *

Nerrik and Joav found Lomis Nortwood, the proprietor and barkeep of Sarls Bend Inn, embroiled in a heated discussion with a few of the town guards outside of their barracks. Nerrik pulled Lomis aside and whispered something secretively in his ear, with furtive glances towards the sentries who were distracted by Joav. He had moved to the guards' quarters, and begun rearranging and tidying the exterior façade.

"Well then, why are you whispering? We..." Lomis was hushed with Nerrik's hand clamped swiftly over his mouth, and a glare that demanded silence.

"Seth called for you specifically. Quiet your tongue and go. Now," he whispered, a little more forcefully.

"I'll take my leave then," Lomis addressed the town guard and Nerrik. Joav continued with his obsessive task of making perfect this ramshackle barracks frontage, as Lomis turned and departed.

"Joav. Let's go." Nerrik grunted with impatience.

"Uh-huh," replied Joav, as he reluctantly left the building looking not quite how he'd desired, and joined his older brother. Together, they began to leave as Nerrik turned to address the town guard.

"Gentlemen..."

They muttered parting words to Nerrik and Joav, looking back and forth between the leave-taking pair and

Joav's impressive handywork. They knew not to question Nerrik, as even Perence Morden, the official lawmaker of Sarls Bend, obediently answered to Seth Bellen. As the pair turned out of sight, down the short lane Lomis had entered, the guards relaxed again, and resumed their previous small talk conversation as if this encounter had never occurred, while the two brothers headed for Seth's stables.

* * *

Dressed and lightly packed, Scarlett pulled on her boots and stood to begin her journey to Mills Wall. She planned to arrive before nightfall, as she was aware that Joshua usually became very elusive from this time on through the night. If she could catch him out and about, she could follow him until the failed light gave opportunity for her to strike. The risk in this plan was great, as Scarlett would have a monumental struggle in controlling the bloodlust of The Sacred Blade of Profanity.

Such was the case any time a mark required an instance of stalking. Scarlett would fold Time and Space in such a way, that her presence in any one spot would seem as an afterthought to the observer—as though somebody had just been, yet was no longer there. With an inordinate amount of Time at her fingertips, she had developed this skill of glamour to a point of second nature, despite The Blade's arduous efforts to immerse itself deep in the rich, hot blood of the intended quarry to consciously distract her. Her ability to move amongst crowds sparse or thick, unnoticed in such a way, ensured The Sacred Blade would be able to carry out its feast, and Scarlett could remain effectively anonymous. In the small, close-knit town of Mills Wall, as in the neighbouring settlements, Scarlett was a vaguely familiar presence, yet essentially still unknown. She had resided in these parts now for nigh on fifty years, yet not once had anybody found it odd that she had remained untouched by the influence of age.

Walking out her door and into the unforgiving entanglement of trees and undergrowth, Scarlett and The Sacred Blade Of Profanity set course for their tragic rendezvous with the now condemned, Joshua Melkerin. Swooping down from the branches overhead to circle tightly above and around Scarlett, her familiars—the ravens, greeted her in a jubilant display of chatter. In fifty years, the ravens had prevailed, just as Scarlett. They seemed also to remain unaffected with age and untouched by time. On countless occasions, Scarlett had witnessed the birds slipping in and out between this world and another, and more often than not, this would herald the next feast of The Blade.

Scarlett had affectionately named the birds Huginn and Muninn; in reference to the two ravens of the Norse god, Odin. Thought and Memory…it seemed apt to Scarlett, and she even fancied the birds perhaps to be the *true* Huginn and Muninn. As it was attested that Odin gave the two ravens the ability to speak, Scarlett was able to understand the seemingly unintelligible vocabulary of Huginn and Munnin as easily and literally as any human tongue. Scarlett was well-versed in many languages and cultures, as well as those of several different worlds and realms. Her propensity for comprehension was impeccable; another result of The Sacred Blade's influence.

They settled to perch; Muninn on her left shoulder, while Huginn took pause atop Scarlett's hooded head, as she stepped and moved through the twisted, ancient trees with an ease that left the birds unruffled and secure in their respective perches. As she proceeded, Huginn and Muninn honed in on her intent, and they travelled through Mellowood Forest as one.

CHAPTER 3

Marnard Gray trembled almost imperceptibly beneath Jahl-Rin's large, rough hand as he re-lived in his mind, the life shattering event that had very recently occurred. The now moderately drunken bandit chief had taken a morbid liking to him, after brutally slaying both of Marnard's parents. The young farmhand had walked into the barn alongside his sizeable residence, to see his mother face down in a pool of her own blood, and Jahl-Rin crouched over his father, drawing a long curved knife across the violently struggling man's throat—his gurgling screams were still very fresh in the ears of Marnard—as he stood with bated breath, nervously by his captor...

Marnard had charged at Jahl-Rin in a blind fury, wildly swinging the wood chopping axe he held in his hands and screaming like a madman, as he ran across the barn towards his freshly dead father, and the monster who had just taken his parent's lives. Jahl-Rin rose quickly and turned to face his irrational assailant front on. A cruel smile spread slowly across his features, displaying the blood and what looked like tiny morsels of the flesh of Marnard's lifeless mother. He continued his advance, but at a decreased and indecisive pace. The wild swinging replaced with a fumbling effort to get a secure grip on the axe, and the insane battle howl fading into nothing, Marnard came face to face with the most terrifying human being he had ever encountered in his nineteen years. Nevertheless, as though time ceased for some moments and the horrific reality of the injustice that lay evident around him sunk in, Marnard, with renewed rage, stepped forward purposefully and gave one almighty swing towards Jahl-Rin's neck. The killer turned slightly and slapped the axe aside, causing the boy to lose his grip on the weapon, along with his balance. Marnard sprawled across the floor, flat on his face with arms outstretched, to unsuccessfully break his fall.

Jahl-Rin let out a loud, short laugh, as he stooped to pick up the discarded lad by the scruff of his neck. As he dragged him to his feet, Marnard started to struggle and swing blindly, in a vain attempt to free himself from this monster. Jahl-Rin cast him back to the ground, as though he were tossing away an unwanted bone. Marnard jumped instantly to his feet, turned to Jahl-Rin with a look of enraged defiance, and once again charged. Somewhat amused and slightly impressed by the boy's pluck, Jahl-Rin caught Marnard's impending punch by the in comparison scrawny forearm, and swung Marnard hard into a solid support beam, rendering him instantly unconscious. Satisfied that the boy wasn't about to get up again anytime soon, Jahl-Rin turned back to finish what he had started. Finger-tapping his numb lower lip thoughtfully, he stood for some moments in appreciation of his own violent deeds, as he gazed across to the woman he had recently violated…

* * *

Whilst inspecting the premises in the prospect of a possible ransack, Jahl-Rin had spotted Marnard's mother entering the barn with a bucket in hand. He quickly followed her unawares into the spacious building, and silently closed in behind the oblivious woman. In the last instant, she felt his presence and turned—but it was too late.

As she opened her mouth to cry out, Jahl-Rin grabbed her roughly to him and planted his foul mouth on hers. Catching her tongue in his teeth, he savagely ripped it from her mouth, before sending a rock solid fist crashing down on the terrified woman's nose. As she crumbled to the floor in a whimpering, agonised heap, Jahl-Rin chewed greedily and swallowed the treat, before descending and forcing her around onto her stomach, pulling up her skirts and roughly tearing the undergarment from her. Taking her from behind, Jahl-Rin viciously raped Marnard's mother, who was unable to scream for help. Holding her hair, he repeatedly slammed the helpless woman's face into the ground, fucking her relentlessly until he felt her body convulse. As he anticipated his impending release, Jahl-Rin lunged his gaping jaws onto her jugular, and tore out the side of her neck.

…Standing slowly as he buckled his belt, Jahl-Rin heard a piercing, high pitched ring; a split second before the impact to the back of his skull was apparent. Marnard's father had walked in just as Jahl-Rin had completed this atrocity, and was struck momentarily still with shock at what he witnessed. A monster, rising from his inert wife, who lay in blood and vitally exposed. He quietly crouched to pick up a large stick that lay at his feet, and crept towards Jahl-Rin, before landing a hefty blow to the back of this repulsive trespasser's head. Mildly stunned, but more annoyed by such a cowardly attack, Jahl-Rin turned slowly to see the stick returning in full swing. He simply lowered his head in a slight nod and allowed the stick to snap in two across his forehead, then answered with a forward stomping kick to the large, but aging man's stomach.

"That was not very fucken smart now, was it?" Jahl-Rin spat venomously. The man lay curled in a ball and fighting for breath, as his aggressor advanced upon him with an onset of indignant wrath. He kicked the prone man hard in the face, flinging him across the floor onto his back, and then continued to kick him as though he were a small stone, all the way across the floor of the barn. The battered fellow raised his hand in a gesture of surrender and pleaded for his life.

"Please!" He warbled through smashed, bloody teeth and broken jaw. "Why are you doing this?!"

Jahl-Rin didn't reply but drew his curved knife, dropped to grab the panicking farmer by the front of his hair, then proceeded to tear open his throat.

***

Marnard was certain he had heard his father's voice, and almost certain that something was not right. He had run into the barn from the woodpile around the side; his suspicion had been precise...terribly precise. The vision he beheld, Marnard Gray would be haunted by for the rest of his life. As he slowly returned to consciousness, Jahl-Rin had already finished cutting the farmer's most vital organ from his chest, and was sitting to Marnard's left, leaning on the barn wall and casually eating his father's heart. All he could do at that moment was lay and scream in impotence and devastation, as Jahl-Rin chuckled here and there while continuing his feed, but that moment passed quick, and Marnard was up and once again charging at this savage intruder. Caught by surprise, Jahl-Rin was too slow to his feet, and Marnard was able to place a hard kick square along the right side of his head, just as he had risen to one foot. Jahl-Rin stumbled and slumped heavily back where he had been sitting.

Obviously, or one would presume, the most rational move at that point would be to run. Abscond without a second thought. This beast was clearly stunned and momentarily down, but he was still conscious, and Marnard fancied that to be his best kick delivered. Yes, he should run, but no. His pure hatred for this man battled fiercely with his intense fear, and began to get the upper hand. He looked around frantically for a weapon and saw his axe, not six quick steps away. In that ample time it took to look, fetch and return, Jahl-Rin had regained his composure fully, and now stood with that psychotic temper of his, rattling his lid and beginning to spill out across his face in twitching, nerve damaged grimaces of the most heinous evil.

"You bastard!" Marnard wailed, as he trembled with fear-ridden adrenaline; axe held firmly in both hands and up by his right shoulder, primed for attack. "I'LL FUCKEN KILL YOU!"

He took two lunging paces and swung a perfectly horizontal arc across the monster's mid-section, but Jahl-Rin merely stepped back on the swing, his vest catching the keen of the axe with a ripping gash, then forward again on the follow through. As he passed the boy, he turned and wrapped his tree trunk of an arm around Marnard's throat and pulled him close, pinning his arms to his sides with his remaining trunk.

"I don't think I'll kill you, boy. I think I'll let you live," Jahl-Rin growled quietly in Marnard's ear. "You impressed me there, with that display of guts. You have a strong spirit, lad. I must break it. Mummy and Daddy are gone, and you now belong to me. Understand? Daddy was a precious waste of my time, but Mummy was at least a good fuck." Marnard slowly turned his eye to see Jahl-Rin's eyeball just a hair's breadth away, staring with malicious intent. "As she was dying by my hand, boy… She was the Best. Fuck. Of. All." He emphasised each word in a gravelly voice, so sinister and chilling to skin and bone, it compelled Marnard to shift his gaze swiftly back to the fore as he froze in the monster's terrible embrace.

What do I say to that? He wondered, in a confusing labyrinth of hateful and fear-driven thoughts.

"You do what I tell you to do now, boy. You belong to me. You call me Boss now. Understand?" Jahl-Rin's arm flexed slightly on Marnard's throat when he didn't, or couldn't, respond.

"UNDERSTAND?" Jahl-Rin roared in his ear and continued to squeeze.

"Y-Y-Yes, Yes." Marnard conceded to 'Boss' reluctantly.

"You may not be so hard to break, after all. Hehe. Once you're broken; your body… your spirit… your will… if you prove true and loyal to me, I will put you back together in such a way, as you one day may stand beside me in battle." Jahl-Rin released his new lackey, and spun him around to face him. "What's your name, kid?"

"M-M-Marnard, s-sir. Boss…" Marnard stammered, quickly correcting his error.

"Marnard??" Boss queried, with an amused, mocking tone. "Marnard? Hahaha!! Marnaaaard! Hahahahaha!! Aaah, the fellas are gonna love you, boy!" He patted Marnard's cheek affectionately with his huge cupped hand; Once and twice and SMACK across his face.

"If you ever raise a hand to me, or disobey me in any way, I will kill you where you cower. I will eat your heart like I did your father, and then fuck your corpse like your mother over there. You got that, Marnaaard?"

Marnard stared at the ground, words escaping him as the ringing in his ear subsided gradually. "Marnard?"

* * *

"Marnaaard!" he was torn from his rumination back into his physical presence. "What the hell are ya doin', boy? Are you thinking? You plotting out your little assassination, or maybe escape? Hahaha, don't worry kid. I just be fuckin' with ya. Think all you like. It doesn't hurt to dream." Jahl-Rin had surely broken this terrified lad, and in only four days. Still, he'd held out longer than most did. The kid was resilient.

"Go down into the cellar, boy, and find me a bottle of their finest rum there. I don't know what I was drinkin' but it tasted like piss. You piss in my drink, boy? You tryin' to poison me, Marnaaard? Nah, of course not. Get out of here!"

CHAPTER 4

The little girl sat amongst the trees, humming a haunting tune in chorus with the gathering of otherworldly beings. A host of swirling, vibrant colours accompanied the harmonies put forth by The Prii and young Dera Harke, which infused her with a mild ecstasy. This semi hypnotic state the child was experiencing occurred on a regular basis, and groomed her psyche for a coming lifetime of perilous adventure. Of this, she was blissfully unaware. Dera had not an inkling of what lay in store for her, and simply enjoyed the frivolous company of her friends, unseen by the eyes of uninitiated mortals. Her destiny would one day soon be painfully revealed to her, but for the time being, Dera Harke was just a seemingly average, though unusual, eleven year old child.

Phenoluh Harke stood by her window, gazing thoughtfully across the way to her daughter, who seemed once again to be interacting with unseen company. This had ceased to bother her some time ago, as Dera seemed happiest in these instances. She had long resigned herself to the notion that her child was mute as well as altogether different from other children, though she was grateful for the little girl's inherent happiness.

Phenoluh was reluctant to disturb young Dera, but the child had been playing in the forest for several hours, and she had finished preparing a simple midday feed of hot fresh bread, a steaming vegetable broth, and a small assortment of fruits for them both.

"Dera!" she called from the window. "Come and eat. I have prepared lunch."

The girl shuddered as she returned to normal waking consciousness, and jumped instantly to her feet at the sound of her mother's bidding. Bolting several paces, she stopped, ran back to where she had sat, and retrieved the small mirror she had left in the grass before her, returning in full pace back to the humble cottage.

Dera had been upset earlier, though she couldn't quite put her finger on why. It seemed like trying to hold onto the fading remnants of a dream upon waking; the more she tried to hold on, the quicker it slipped from her grasp. She didn't know how to convey to her mother what she felt, because she didn't know herself. Whilst Phenoluh was going about the daily chores, (she liked to have it all done nice and early when the market was closed, so the rest of the day belonged to herself and Dera) the child slipped out the back door, unnoticed by her mother. She did make a very visual account of being outside though, running past the kitchen window and out across the small field, towards Mellowood Forest. She didn't want to worry Phenoluh, neither by her unfounded unhappiness nor by her dubious whereabouts, so young Dera waited until she was already outside before making sure her mother saw her.

Dera skipped and ran with the mirror she had continuously swiped from Phenoluh's drawer, until her mother had given up and agreed to 'share' it with Dera. She knew the little girl loved it. Yes, Dera did love it—but not for the reason Phenoluh thought it was. She fancied that it reminded Dera of her daddy, when in truth; the child couldn't remember Daddy at all. Phenoluh was all Dera knew. Phenoluh and of course, The Prii.

Already, The Prii had gathered about Dera as she left the cottage, sensing her aura and coming to her aid with curious concern. Dera could be fairly moody at times, but this was something vastly different. This was something of the profane. Her mood brightened considerably and swiftly as The Prii went to work. Cloaking their concern upon arrival, they greeted Dera with an ancient tune named Dan're Dul; said to have been the tune that sprouted the very first seed of the mighty Mellowood Forest. The Prii were masters of vibrational frequencies. They could heal you of your ills with a soothing song, always accompanied by an appropriate colour or blend of colours, permeating the air around them to those that *see*. In saying that, The Prii were just as proficient at disrupting a person's energy body to a point causing death; dulling the senses with blackened smoke that smothers and quickly suffocates for a humane but sure end. A method of drawing the darkness from inside an individual and drowning them in it. Purely a defensive mechanism and never out of malice, The Prii simply meted out justice if it were so due, as an inherent part of their nature. There was no emotional attachment whatsoever.

* * *

It had been quite some time… nine years, since they were compelled to exert this power. When the Mirror was in the hands of another, albeit only briefly. A hunter had stumbled across the Mirror in Mellowood Forest, as he stalked a large deer amidst the trees. Its glimmer caught his keen hunter's eye and as he picked it up, the deer came to a standstill. The Prii had averted its attention, keeping it enthralled and fixed to the spot, as Michael Harke placed the Mirror in his pouch and slowly, quietly drew his bow, taking aim. The deer didn't look at him but straight ahead, presenting a full side on target to the puzzled huntsman. His eye saw where his arrow would strike and he gracefully released, finding his mark with perfect accuracy. The deer screamed and lunged a couple of steps sideways, before stumbling forward and falling down dead. This was an auspicious day for Michael. He now had two things; enough food to feed his beloved family for quite some time, and an inexpensive looking but from the heart gift for his darling wife. The Prii knew his intentions were pure. He would use every part of the animal, and gave it thanks as he cradled its lifeless head in his hands. They had seen this in Michael Harke from the moment he caught sight of the Mirror. In gratitude for taking notice, The Prii gifted Michael with this splendid beast, for which he was in turn a touch confused, yet truly grateful.

Whilst holding his fallen prey and giving it a respectful send off, a second arrow thudded uninvited into the carcass, right beside his own.

"Ay! Get away from that, it's mine. My kill!" Michael looked up to see three men on the embankment to his right and another two directly ahead. The one who had called out and who was obviously the shooter, stepped forward with his hunting bow still in hand.

"The deer died by my hand, sirs. I was giving my respects at such a fortunate affair, when your arrow found its home beside mine. I am sorry, but the deer belongs to me."

In answer to this, another arrow struck the ground, dangerously close to Michael's leg as he squatted by his quarry.

"That's not how we see it, mister. I shot that deer. I have four more people here who agree with me. Now step away from the animal."

Michael stood slowly to see two of the three people on the embankment slink off around behind some thick scrub, presumably to surround him. The burly fellow with the big mouth strode up to Michael with an air of disrespectful nonchalance, stood arrogantly before him, and once again spoke.

"Move!"

"No." Michael stood his ground with the intruder. The adrenaline and fear in him evident in his shaking leg, though his stony gaze remained unmoved, Michael stared down his opponent in challenge.

"No? Hehe... Did ya's hear that, fellas? He said 'No'!" The loudmouth brigand heard no reply from his comrades, for they were nowhere to be seen. "Millen? Basfal! *Where is everybody?*" As the thief turned back to Michael, his mouth suddenly locked open, and his pupils dilated until there was naught left of his eyeballs but black. He felt as though bits of him were being taken out and put back all wrong. No pain, but a terrible fear accompanied this sensation, as horrid tones tugged at his psyche, pulling him under waves of terror incarnate, to suffocate him in the full knowledge and realisation of all of his life's transgressions.

Michael Harke was bewildered by what he had just witnessed. That, and the uncharacteristically co-operative deer he had just shot, coupled with the mysterious disappearance of the other men on the scene, left him wondering if he was lying beneath a tree and dreaming all of this. Coming to the conclusion that he was indeed very much awake, he decided to simply count his blessings, as he awkwardly lifted the heavy deer to place across his broad shoulders, and began the slow walk back to the cottage.

CHAPTER 5

Phenoluh and Dera ate their meal in the customary lack of conversation that accompanied the activities in which they partook together. Phenoluh threw the occasional glance towards her child as she scoffed her food quickly between giggles and beaming smiles. Phenoluh had long since given up asking her child what she found so amusing. Dera seemed happy, and that was all that mattered to her mother. As they continued with their lunch, she nevertheless couldn't help wondering what it was that gave Dera over to these giggling spells. She had grown accustomed to the strange looks and petty whispers among the folk in town, as her daughter displayed all the qualities of one who was 'not quite right up there'. In fact, Dera Harke was highly intelligent and extremely coherent. Some of the townsfolk even boldly fancied the silent and strange young lass to be musing over a devious plot to raze the whole town of Mills Wall to the ground, killing everyone in the process. Such was the mentality of the largely ignorant inhabitants of the town, as well as the general area surrounding these parts—simple folk, with simple hopes, and perhaps, not so simple fears.

Dera, of course, entertained no such notion. Her odd manner and strangeness simply outshone her fundamental innocence, and painted an inaccurate picture of young Dera Harke, to which the majority of Mills Wall's inhabitants reacted by politely, but consistently, being on their way when the child was on the loose in town. Although this distressed Phenoluh, as she was bound to stay by her stall so that they would earn enough to eat for the following day, perhaps it was in fact a godsend that Dera was off on her little adventures, and not by the stall with her. Perhaps it was purely thanks to Dera that the marketplace was always busy and full, no matter the day. If she had indeed stayed by her mother, the market would likely become quiet as the grave, and there would be a lot of firewood to cart back home at day's end. Phenoluh was well loved by all in the town. One of the most likeable and giving that any of them had ever known—but the peculiar behaviour of her daughter, they just could not abide.

Phenoluh stood as they were both finishing, to clear the table. She reached for the loaf, and Dera swiftly snapped her hand down onto the bread. The cutest smile broke at Phenoluh, as Dera slowly with her other hand, reached forward to tear a chunk off, before removing her top hand slowly, and with the other hand, quickly slipping the bread into her loose pocket. A sleight of hand glamour that struck the memory of the sequence of actions from Phenoluh's mind. She picked up the bread and returned Dera's smile. "Beautiful child," she said lovingly, as she turned towards the pantry.

The Prii had shown Dera this and many more magiks over the course of their friendship. A friendship that blurred along the line of apprenticeship. To the child, it was just plain old fun. Always, The Prii would show Dera love and caring support, both in her highs and her lows. The knowledge they would impart to the young girl came to her in music and visual beauty that just had no words to bring comprehension. Dera would simply know. In her body, the vehicle in which Dera Harke walked this plane, she knew at once what to do. The Mirror had taught Dera many things, one of which was being aware of her body as just that. A tool for her spirit to work with. Just as The Mirror was an extension of Dera's hand, her hand was an extension of her soul. The joyous and frivolous nature of The Prii ensured that Dera found a great peace and enjoyment in learning what they had to teach. After nine years, at eleven and a half years old, she was already quite adept at several things that would be deemed unnatural by average folk. As Dera just 'knew' these things, to her, they were completely natural. She understood that she knew and could do things that nobody she was acquainted with, let alone had ever seen, could accomplish. She was careful—even with her own mother—not to expose her inherent skill, which was a skill in itself. In this aspect, Dera had indeed become most adept.

* * *

    Seth made his way past the limits into Sarls Bend and, as immediately as was not too painfully obvious, slunk down the first pathway off the main and back through the winding narrow streets, towards his stables. He had been careful to avoid the Sarls Bend Inn, and the bandits that had taken it for their length of stay. However long that may be, Seth didn't want to guess. He and his crew were getting them out of there before nightfall, one way or another. He had even contemplated locking them in there and just torching the place. Be done with it. Done with them. Everyone else had been chased out of there—at least, he hoped so. He would have to somehow find that out. Burning the place down aside, a hostage situation would only blow everything to astronomical proportions, ultimately leading to a bloodbath involving innocent folk.

    "Dammit! This plan isn't coming together well at all..." Seth kicked a small rock along the pathway, as he tried to find new solutions to new possible outcomes. "When I get everyone back at the stables, we'll have quite a few sharp minds to rub together. These bastards have to go..."

* * *

Marnard searched lazily through the cellar for the boss's rum. He didn't know how to spell, but he knew the shape of the word RUM very well. His dad used to like his rum. In moderation, of course. Never in the day time, and only just before heading off to bed for the night, after a full day in the fields. Marnard shared the same workload, but he was only nineteen. In his prime, or so he liked to think. Dad was old. At least fifty. Still, Marnard Gray was a strong and respectful lad, of whom his father was proud.

'I like a rum, son. It helps to rest my weary bones of a night. Get me the bottle there, will you?' Marnard remembered handing the bottle of rum to his father, who took it by the neck, clasping Marnard's hand to the bottle. Pulling off the cork, he told him,

'This, Marnard, is Power. People who abuse Power become slaves to it.' Taking a cup in his free hand, he tipped Marnard's hand up to slowly and purposefully fill it with the clear liquid. At three quarters full, Marnard's father halted the pour, and took the bottle from his son's hand, extending the cup to him in its place.

'Take this, but sip it slowly. Taste its fire and respect its Power. Never abuse this Power, Marnard. Always be wise in your decisions, and always be true to yourself. Practise this, and you will go far in life. Your mother and I have done well in raising a fine young man, son. We are very proud of you, and trust the decisions you make in life will always be the right ones that you know in your soul. We're always here for you son. *son.. son... son....*'

Marnard jolted back to reality and saw that he had in his hands, the very bottle that his father shared with him not two years ago. Well, not *the* very bottle but the same label, nonetheless. *Fuck him, he's not getting any of this*, thought Marnard, as he began to look where he must have unconsciously found the rum. Hopefully to find one to replace this one. This one, he was going to stash for himself. And he would respect that Power. That Power would free him from his bonds of captivity, and hopefully from his horrific past. He knew his father was only using rum as a metaphor, but his message rang true to Marnard; more so now than ever before. He uncorked the bottle and took a shallow swig before corking it once again.

"That was for you, dad." Marnard saluted his late patriarch, aloud but not loud. "Yes!" he quietly exclaimed, discovering a shelf full of bottles with the letters RUM on them. His RUM would not be missed…and hopefully not found…

Marnard kicked some of the hay that was scattered over the cellar floor, presumably there to absorb the obvious smelling dampness of the subterranean room filled with liquor. Making a tiny pile, unnoticeable in a corner near to the bottom of the stairs, Marnard placed his sacred symbol of Power in amongst it so it was no longer visible, and blending with the shadows. He walked slowly to perform the menial and thoroughly demeaning task of fetching drink for his parents' killer. He'd watched his beloved father die at this cannibal's hand, but by Hells, he had raped Marnard's mother and told him, several times already and in great detail, what he had done to her.

At this thought, Marnard felt the rum turn in his stomach, and start to burn a trail up through his chest, slowing its ascent as it crept into his throat. These scars were excruciatingly fresh, and Jahl-Rin made damn sure those scars began healing when Jahl-Rin said they did. He managed to supress the vomit, but the rum had churned with his empty stomach juices and erupted all through his body, burning like a volcano and taking his breath away. Marnard started to feel the subtle effects of his meagre partake. Not drunk, but affected. He reasoned his following sensation to be what they called 'liquid courage', as he wanted to once again charge wildly up the stairs with Jahl-Rin's bottle, and smash it over the gigantic maggot's head.

His reason was still firmly intact, however.

He thought it most wise to acknowledge that he had made a decision. This decision would spawn many more decisions, which may either aid or hinder the fruition of the original decision made. Obviously, to rush up there swinging a bottle would be the terminal act of a fool, and Marnard Gray was no fool. He would allow the plan to grow organically, and bide his time until the time was Now. Escape was the ultimate objective, but if it meant he had to kill in order to succeed, then so be it. Visions of his resolution filled him with horror... gory, terrible horror. He would continually try and play out the hero role in his head, but the inevitable truth would keep devouring him, piling upon him like cannibalistic, smothering mutations of life. He would have to wait and either, (more preferably) slip away unnoticed, or fight his way out and run for dear life- should he escape in one piece that is. The time at that point was not Now, so Marnard reluctantly returned to Jahl-Rin with his damn rum. Jahl-Rin's whipping boy. His getter. His godsdamned slave! Marnard felt his rage struggling with his will, thankfully to no avail, as he approached his captor from behind. Visions of striding up behind him; the corner of the table he sat at, in a perfect angle to smash the bottle and in the same swing, bring the jagged glass tearing through the jugular. He could do it easily before anybody could stop him...Jahl-Rin would be dead.

"C'mon, boy. You're not at mummy and daddy's funeral march. Get here with that bottle now, Marnaaard!"

Eyes downcast, Marnard hurried across the room to where Jahl-Rin sat, and presented the boss with his damn rum. "S-sorry Boss."

"Where were you? I've grown fucken sober waitin' for my rum! Give it here, you fucken little..." Jahl-Rin snatched the bottle from the boy's hand, looking at him with suspicion for the downward gaze. "Look at me, boy. Look me in the fucken eye."

Marnard raised his head slowly to meet Jahl-Rin's gaze. He couldn't hide the brief glimmer of defiance in his otherwise submissive glances, which bounced out of his control from one scrutinizing eye to another, making him dizzy and wanting to vomit all over again. No matter, within his obedience or his apparent submissive servitude, Jahl-Rin caught that fleeting glare. Defiance, attitude…rebellion that could cause unease in the ranks would be a problem. Marnard's error was answered with the back of Jahl-Rin's fist across the side of his head, and he fell quickly to the ground, vomiting out of consciousness.

CHAPTER 6

As Joshua peered towards the early afternoon sun, he decided it was about time to prepare for his rendezvous with Jahl-Rin. It was a two day walk as the crow flies, and Jahl-Rin was not one to put up with tardiness. His mysterious proposal had Joshua intrigued, and he surely did not want to pass up any opportunity the bandit chief may present him with. If he wasn't there at the agreed upon time and place, Jahl-Rin and his crew would simply move on, and Joshua would miss out on a potential windfall. This would also jeopardise any future dealings with the brute, as the bandit was a 'one chance only' sort, who dealt in business solely with those he deemed reliable and, in accordance with his own twisted ethics, trustworthy. Joshua prided himself on these qualities—qualities that were subject to his own self-deceiving interpretation.

Joshua proceeded into the house to dress and gather for the long trip ahead. The eye of The Blade followed via The Watcher with urgency. They weren't going to get to Mills Wall in time. *"Scarlett, we must change course. Joshua Melkerin will be leaving for Sarls Bend shortly. Perhaps we can intercept him under cover of Mellowood. We must be swift though."*

Scarlett immediately cut an angle left and picked up her pace; Huginn and Muninn holding their perches unflinchingly, whilst several miles away, Joshua left Mills Wall through the Eastern Gate, to traverse the well-trodden path amid Mellowood's more accessible top end. He still felt he was being watched, and the notion that somebody was following his every move unsettled Joshua so much that he practically ran from the town gate to the concealment of the forest, not more than a hundred paces away.

Joshua was an exceptionally greedy individual. Fear was a dominant emotion in his life, as his line of work would dictate. He had grown accustomed to this sentiment, however. Learned to embrace it even. Joshua Melkerin never allowed fear to get in the way of making some serious coin, and serious coin was always to be had when dealing with Jahl-Rin. He impatiently pushed aside the dread feeling of being watched, and turned his thoughts to what lucrative enterprise the bandit had in wait. From Joshua's past experience with Jahl-Rin, he was certain he would have to get his hands dirty to reap the reward, but just how dirty this time?

He was startled out of his thoughts and very nearly out of his skin, by a rustle in the trees to his left. A huge raven took flight from a fairly low branch and swooped at Joshua, causing him to duck awkwardly and curse loudly. The large bird cawed and cackled with an apparently mocking tone, as it rose above the trees to be joined by another raven. Together, they flew off to the west and seemed to disappear into thin air, leaving Joshua visibly shaken and perturbed. He quickened his pace along the path through Mellowood Forest. Two more hours and he would be clear of this cursed place. Mellowood always gave Joshua the horrors. He abhorred the forest, but it was the quickest and shortest way between where he was and where he must arrive.

* * *

Seth Bellen rounded the final bend leading up to his sprawling property. He could see his party gathered by the stables, sitting near the gates and talking amongst themselves. He broke into a trot towards the group. He was on a mission, yet he was still at a loss as to how he and his deputies were to carry it out. Hopefully they had come up with a sound plan, and weren't simply engaging in idle banter.

"What news of the inn, Nortwood?" he called out as he approached the group. "I want numbers, man. Who, besides these bastards is still in there?"

Lomis stood to address Seth, as he removed his wide brimmed hat, and turned it in his hands nervously.

"Nobody, to my knowledge, sir. Nobody but those treacherous brigands. I am beside myself, thinking what they are doing to my establishment! I can only guess. They sent me packing last night with naught but the clothes on my back! I had to sleep in the godsdamn street!" Seth waited for Lomis to finish his rant.

"Just the facts, Nortwood. I don't have the time or the care to hear your laments. How many of them?" he retorted with more than a hint of impatience.

"Then nobody, Mr. Bellen, sir. I was the last of our own to be ejected from the place, and I doubt greatly that anyone would have the hide to go within twenty paces of the front doors. I would say there are about fifteen or so."

"Good," said Seth. "Then we burn that fucking place to the ground with those bastards in it."

"What?! NO! My heart and soul is in that inn! My livelihood! What will I do? Where will I go? Where will I live?!"

Seth glared at the distraught innkeeper. "Shut your mouth, Nortwood. What would you suggest then? Shall we take them on in battle? Will you lead the charge to save your precious inn, and drive them from our fair town? No, I don't think so. We barricade them in, and burn it and them to ash."

Lomis began again to protest, but a look that would

melt stone from Bellen the thug shut him down instantly. He started to walk away, then turned back to Seth, thought better of it, and continued to mill around aimlessly like a lost child. It was pointless and certainly perilous to pursue any kind of argument with Seth.

"There is an alternative," the young woman, Neesa Tarmer spoke up. "Perhaps we could send Joav in to draw them out and away from the inn. There is nobody in all of Sarls Bend who can run like him. If we spread out through the town and take to hiding, we could pick them off from all directions with bows."

"Huh?" Joav looked around at the mention of his name.

"Like Hell!" Nerrik piped up. "My brother may be an idiot, and in your eyes expendable, but he is my brother, not some damn fall guy for your plots and plans. Out of the question!"

"She has a point, Nerrik," Lomis interjected, in the hope of saving his inn from devastation. "Joav is indeed quick on his feet. Jahl-Rin and the rest are drunk as sailors. There is not a chance they could keep pace with him."

"Quick as he may be, could he outrun a flying dagger? Or a damned arrow? No. You are not sending my brother to his death to save your shitty booze house! Out of the question godsdammit! Seth?"

Seth took in what had been put forward and squatted down in thought for a few moments, before once again rising to his full stature in a display of authority. "Well, does anybody else have a more suitable suggestion? None of us are expendable. We are not sending Joav, or anyone of you for that matter, into harm's way. Time is getting away from us. If nobody can come up with another option, then I'm sorry, Lomis. We burn it..."

"What the hell does time have to do with anything? We are talking about my inn here! My home of more than thirty years! As loath as I may be to have this filth in my home, I won't stand by and watch all I have in this world turn to ashes! Can't we just wait it out? Surely they will leave before long." Lomis was desperately pleading his case to an unmovable Seth Bellen.

"And then what, Nortwood? I won't have just anyone walking into my town and taking over whenever they see fit to do so. If we let them be, then we may as well change the name of the town to something like Cowards godsdamn Bend! Ok. Nobody else? It's settled then. We burn the inn and be done with the lot of 'em."

Your town? Like Hell, you pompous bastard! Lomis Nortwood was livid but dared not speak his mind. He slumped down against the fence, broken and defeated.

"We will all pitch in and build you a new inn, Lomis," Neesa offered in a consoling tone.

"It wouldn't be the same, Neesa, but thank you nonetheless," Lomis replied with a tear in his eye. "My stock climbs into the thousands. I could never replace what I've built up over the decades. I will be ruined, to be sure." The rest of the deputies just sat in silence. Nobody had any better plan to offer, and it seemed the bully coward of Sarls Bend would have his way after all.

* * *

Marnard stirred on the dirty floor, to the sounds of a heated argument that grew in pitch and volume to a painful cacophony, as his consciousness returned. Nursing a swollen jaw and burning pain in his ear, he slowly picked himself up from the ground, and looked over to where the commotion was taking place. One of Jahl-Rin's men lay out cold, bleeding profusely from his face. Standing either side of the unfortunate fellow, was Goatus and a man he remembered by the name of Kohass. Another behemoth, seething with rage at the calmly smiling Goatus, whose demeanour threatened to escalate the standoff between himself and Kohass into a new bloody clash of violence. Kohass was screaming at Goatus, an accusing finger threatening to poke a hole clear through his face, while the remainder of Jahl-Rin's crew cheered both sides on with bottles, both empty and full, being hurled back and forth across the room. Goatus simply stood there defiantly; his face a terrible mask of leering amusement.

The boy sat still and watched as the two giants faced off. He didn't fancy Kohass stood a chance, big as he was. He had seen what Goatus Of Torment was capable of, and would have even bet in his favour if the opponent were none other than Jahl-Rin himself. He figured the unconscious man between them had been victim to the mighty Goatus, but hadn't a clue what had brought him to this unfortunate outcome. All eyes were on the feuding pair, and Marnard wondered if this might be his chance to slip away and be free of these monsters.

"Back among the living, eh, Marnard? You know why I smacked you down, yes?"

Jahl-Rin put a swift end to that thought, and Marnard shrank away from his tormentor with a mix of terror and hidden hatred. He knew exactly why, yet didn't know how to respond, so he kept silent. He was careful not to let slip any more untoward glances at Jahl-Rin as the menacing figure loomed over him.

"Cat got ya tongue, boy? Whatever you were thinkin' earlier, I suggest you perish that thought permanently. I told ya what I would do, should you challenge me. Your eyes betrayed the raised fist I warned you about back in the barn. I let ya off lightly this instance. Next time, you're my dinner." Jahl-Rin strode off towards the impending brawl, leaving Marnard shivering in his place. *"What the fuck's goin' on here?* Calm down, you screamin' idiots!"

Fight or flight kicked in hard, and Marnard was torn between turning tail straight out the door of the inn, and running for dear life to gods know where, never to return to Sarls Bend, or being an obedient pet and staying put. He silently tore strips from his unsteady mind, with how completely at Jahl-Rin's mercy he had allowed himself to become. The self-loathing was making him feel ill. He quietly got up and made his way to the door of the cellar. He would leave, but not without his RUM. Descending the stairs, he could hear the shouting continue and hurried to where he had stashed his bottle, then ran light-footed back to the top and stopped by the door. The standoff seemed to have grown to three now, with Jahl-Rin joining the fray, and all of the bandits preoccupied with what was transpiring. Marnard clutched the bottle behind his back, and began the hazardous walk towards the entrance to Sarls Bend Inn.

Just outside and across the quiet main street, Seth Bellen, the Sarls Bend coward, watched from behind the safety of a large cart as Nerrik, Joav, Neesa, and a young lad named Garrin crept warily towards the front of the inn. They carried thick wooden poles that they were to lodge up against the outwardly turning doors and across the three large shuttered windows, in an attempt to trap Jahl-Rin and his lot inside. Seth had sent two others, Petri Dahbl and Arliss Bregg, to the side windows with the same task. Lomis Nortwood had refused to have any part in the terrible plot, and had elected to stay behind at Seth's stables.

Marnard reached the doors, unnoticed by the bandit crew, and flung them open just as the four deputies stepped onto the landing. Marnard stopped dead with rum in hand, and stared at Nerrik and co. for a moment before tearing off to the side of the building, bowling over Arliss Bregg as he bolted up the street. Seth jumped out from behind the cart with a yell, and the four sent to barricade the inn stood confused at the sight of the young farmhand's surprise escape. Jahl-Rin and the rest of the outlaw gang all halted their in house dispute at this interruption, and rushed towards the doors as one entity. Blades, clubs, and an assortment of terrible weaponry drawn, they poured out of the inn like a revolting wave, much to the dismay of Seth Bellen's disorganised posse.

Jahl-Rin at the fore, Neesa Tarmer was the first to taste steel. She fell beneath his swinging knife arm, which opened up the side of her face and nearly took her jaw clean from her, as the blade slashed through flesh and muscle. The other three in her company froze momentarily in shocked awe at the vicious assault, before scattering in blind panic for whatever sanctuary they could find. Seth remained hidden behind the cart and watched, as these monsters chased down his deputies with bloodthirsty howls, enjoying themselves immensely. This was what they lived for. The thrill of violence and terror, be it a rival gang or, as in this case, a town full of helpless folk.

"*Marnaaard*! *Where is that fucking whelp*? Spread out, men. Kill every last one of these maggots! I want that boy!" Jahl-Rin was beside himself with rage, as he hurled his knife at Arliss, who had recovered from his collision with Marnard far too slowly to make any kind of effective escape. He had gotten to his feet only to be knocked immediately back down—the dirty, rusting dagger thudding heavily into his chest. Seth saw his opportunity and slipped around the side of the general store, sprinting down the side street towards his stables. Joav was a speck in the distance, running for his life and hoping his brother had also managed escape….he hadn't. Nerrik lay in the middle of the street with his head twisted at an unnatural angle. Goatus Of Torment had fallen upon him in three quick, giant steps and landed a blow on the back of Nerrik's neck, breaking it with ease and killing him instantly.

"Every house! Every building!" Jahl-Rin screamed maniacally. "Find Marnard and destroy anyone you cross!

This town is finished!"

Turning his attention to the few people who had come outside the mailhouse to see what the commotion was about, had heard the beast's chilling words and immediately ran back inside the building, Jahl-Rin charged towards them with the pole Nerrik had been carrying. Moments after entering the mailhouse, bloodcurdling screams chorused with enraged howls of "Marnaaard!" which brought more townsfolk out of their homes, only to be brutally cut down by Jahl-Rin's men. If Perence Morden had been in town, perhaps things may have been different. Maybe if he were there with the real deputies of Sarls Bend, its inhabitants may have had a small sliver of hope. The four sentries who stayed behind were a token, if nothing more, and actually elected to make themselves scarce as the massacre commenced; retreating to the barracks to hide and wait it out instead. How could he have known though, that his normally peaceful town and the people dwelling therein, were to be terrorised by the invading mob of cut-throats.

Unfortunately, he and several of his men had been called away to meet with the Trade Council across the bay in Terrinus, to negotiate current sanctions incurred by Seth Bellen. The loudmouth had been involved in a very public disagreement with the head fishmonger in Terrinus. Seth's arrogance and pride resulted in his order that none from Sarls Bend would give the fishing village their custom or coin. This was causing a great inconvenience for both, as the two settlements had traded goods across The Bay of Solace for generations, and essentially kept each other in business. The bay was vast but sparsely populated, and the seclusion of both town and village meant they relied heavily on eachother for prosperity. It seemed Seth Bellen had a lot to answer for…. and now much more so.

Seth was just about to reap the beginnings of his comeuppance as he looked to the skies over the buildings ahead. Massive billows of black smoke rose high over rooftops, coming from what appeared to be his stables. Lomis Nortwood was suitably enraged by Seth's heartless decision to destroy his inn, and took it upon himself to repay the deed in full. He had thrown open the gates, releasing all of Seth's horses before setting fire to the stables. The flames took quickly to the wooden structure with bales of hay scattered throughout, and within mere seconds, the stables were completely engulfed. Seth knew instantly what had transpired and by whom. His sprint increased twofold, although he knew there was nothing he could do to save his stables.

"Damn you, Nortwood!" he panted as he ran. "Damn you to all the hells! I'll have your head when I get hold of you!"

* * *

Marnard slowly swigged his bottle of rum as he was ferried across the bay to Terrinus. His escape had been narrow indeed. Almost thwarted by the townsfolk of Sarls Bend for reasons he may never become aware of. He didn't care. He was free of Jahl-Rin's tyranny and that was all that mattered to him. Terrinus was the only place outside of his home across the bay that he had visited, and he was nervous and apprehensive of what his life now held in store for him. The ferryman left Marnard to his troubled thoughts, and dutifully took him to his destination in silence.

At the port in Terrinus, Perence Morden and his men waited to return to Sarls Bend, completely unaware of what was taking place back home. With Marnard nowhere to be found, the folk of Sarls Bend were paying dearly at the hands of Jahl-Rin and his crew, who slaughtered nearly all without mercy. The lawmaker, Perence, would be returning to a relative ghost town, with only a scattered few managing to evade the band of cutthroats…not to mention, the cutthroats themselves.

CHAPTER 7

Joshua broke from Mellowood without further incident and continued across the Three Mark Plains, to the well-travelled road leading to Terrinus. The ravens had returned to Scarlett, who, despite her fast gait, was still several hours away from Joshua Melkerin. They relayed Joshua's position and current course to her before resuming their perches on head and shoulder. Scarlett held pace as Huginn and Muninn guided her south, south-east, to hopefully intercept Joshua before he made it to the bayside village. If he were to get across the Bay of Solace, Scarlett would have to await his return in Terrinus, or follow across on the next boat to Sarls Bend.

The Three Mark Plains were notorious for bandits and other unsavoury characters who preyed upon unwary travellers, but Joshua was unconcerned, as many of these outlaw folk had, at one time or another, procured certain favours from him in various forms. Joshua was well known in these parts as someone who was not unforthcoming in matters of a dubious nature. He was considered one of them, and well respected in these circles. Though he wasn't an overly intimidating fellow, his persuasive powers of diplomacy, and willingness to partake in nearly any unscrupulous venture, had earned him free passage to walk at liberty and without consequence in this part of the land.

Scarlett, on the other hand, would be considered fair game, as her anonymity kept her from their acquaintance. The Sacred Blade Of Profanity knew this, and revelled in the thought of a chance meeting with said characters.

"Joshua Melkerin will keep, Scarlett," said The Sacred Blade, hearing Scarlett's thoughts, and feeling her frustration build at the elusiveness of Joshua. *"Patience has its own dividends, Scarlett. He is up to something, and perhaps it's better that we allow him time to draw other players into the fold. It has been too long since I have fed and I am feeling a touch greedy."*

There were sinister undertones lurking in the voice of The Blade that made Scarlett shudder. It was true that nearly an entire moon cycle had passed since their last kill. That one had been particularly gruesome. Scarlett had lost control over The Blade Of Power, and had given herself over to the bloodlust completely. So very out of manner for Scarlett, who was extremely meticulous and methodical in every action she performed; especially when it involved The Sacred Blade Of Profanity. She had always maintained that necessary detachment…at least for the most part. The early days of their collaboration had been a different story, of course. The 'teething' stage had been very difficult for Scarlett and, as with every host The Blade had shared time with, awkward for both—to say the least. She had, however, adapted quickly and learned the many secrets of The Sacred Blade, with an ease that astounded even The Blade itself. Scarlett was by far the most adept wielder of The Sacred Blade Of Profanity, since its creation many thousands of years ago. Lately, however, she felt her grasp slipping and this worried her greatly. Scarlett was beginning to tire from the demands of The Blade. The burden was growing by the day, and she struggled to retain control of her own will, let alone that of The Sacred Blade of Profanity.

* * *

Joshua stopped to rest briefly after walking an hour

or so in the hot sun. There was nowhere to take refuge from the heat, but he needed to drink and eat some of the food he had brought for the journey. He still had quite a distance to travel once reaching the road to Terrinus, and he hoped to have the good fortune of finding someone with a mode of transport other than foot to share the way south. From his position in the plains, Joshua could see for miles in each direction the road stretched, and was somewhat disappointed that the road was empty. Still, in the time it would take to walk that far, there was always the chance somebody may happen his way. As the sweat stung his eyes, he began to miss the cool shade of Mellowood Forest, as much as it pained him to admit it. His excess paunch made the heat so much more uncomfortable.

After a frugal snack of bread and dried meat, he continued across the plain towards the long, wide road. His pack was getting heavier as the journey wore on, and he wished to the gods he was already at the Sarls Bend Inn, enjoying a fine wine and something more substantial to eat than bread and dried meat. In anticipation of the long haul, he had elected to pack as lightly as possible, but felt he had still brought along too much. Nevertheless, he stood awkwardly and continued on his way. He wouldn't get there any quicker by merely wishing it to be so.

* * *

Joav sobbed in exhaustion. He hadn't stopped running, or even looked back to see if he was being pursued. He had a terrible gut feeling that his brother hadn't made it out of there, and was loath to think what those bastards were doing to him. It would have been little consolation to know that Nerrik hadn't felt a thing. Goatus Of Torment had made very short work of sending him to the afterlife with his huge club, which had near decapitated the fleeing Nerrik. Joav struggled with his mind as to whether he should return to Sarls Bend, in the slight hope of rescuing his brother from Jahl-Rin and his men. He was terrified by the thought of being captured or killed himself, and was at a loss about what to do next. Satisfied that he hadn't been followed, he dropped onto the grass and let his mind go blank. This was his failsafe way of coping when he felt overwhelmed, which happened a lot for poor Joav.

He didn't have the mental capacity of his elder sibling, whom he relied upon for quite a lot. Nerrik was a fairly supportive brother, even though he would often get frustrated at Joav and his unusual behaviours. He couldn't help it, though he knew he was acting like an idiot. This would, in turn, frustrate Joav as well. He just wanted to be normal like everyone else. Unfortunately, this wasn't so. He had been different from birth, often acting on impulses that were beyond his control, and that left him as one who people would invariably take advantage of. Nerrik was always beating folk in defence of his idiot brother. He really was good to him. Thoughts began to creep slowly back into his mind, and Joav erupted in hysterical tears at the thought of losing Nerrik forever. After much hesitation, he decided to go back to Sarls Bend and try to find him.

* * *

Lomis was nowhere in sight as Seth Bellen reached the open gates. His horses were also absent, bar one, which stood in the field adjoining the stables, nervously chewing on grass. Seth felt his knees weaken and seething rage fill him to bursting at the sight before him. Lomis Nortwood was a dead man as far as Seth was concerned. He just had to find him first. The stables were burnt beyond saving, but he still had a steed. He made his way into the field, and approached his still startled animal with caution. He didn't want to frighten it any more than it already was, so he trod softly, beckoning the horse with gentle clicking sounds and reassuring words as he got closer. Without saddle or bridle, he hoped coaxing it back through the open gate wouldn't prove too much of a task. A spooked horse could be very unpredictable, so he would have to first calm the beast before attempting to bring it in. He hoped there would be some riding gear left undamaged by the arson, so that he could saddle up and hunt down Nortwood. Little did he know that Lomis Nortwood was now far from this place on another of Seth's prize steeds, heading west around the perimeter of the vast Bay Of Solace.

Lomis had no idea his inn had remained standing and unscathed. He felt minimal satisfaction in his vengeful act of burning down Seth Bellen's stables, as he spurred the magnificent horse on along the bay. He had made sure he nabbed Bellen's fastest and most favoured before turning the rest loose. Now he was riding like the wind to gods know where, as long as it was far from Sarls Bend, and the heartless coward who had presumably taken everything Lomis Nortwood owned. His heart was heavy at the loss he imagined, and he felt no reason to ever return. He was one of the lucky few. If he ever were to return, he would find his inn standing, unscathed in the midst of a very sparsely populated town.

* * *

The ferry docked at Terrinus and Marnard jumped shakily onto the pier. He had consumed a little more rum than he had planned whilst lost in his thoughts and was a touch inebriated.

Perence Morden caught the boy and steadied him, as his men boarded the boat.

"You look a bit worse for weather, boy." Morden released his grip on Marnard when he was sure he'd found his feet.

"Yes, sir. Yes, I am," replied Marnard. "I wouldn't

recommend travelling back across the water."

"Haha! We make this trip regularly, son. Without a belly full of liquor, I might add." The staunch lawman had obviously misunderstood the lad.

"That's not what I meant, sir. My parents are dead. Murdered by Jahl-Rin and his band of thugs. I fear the same fate has befallen many, if not *all* the folk of Sarls Bend. I managed to escape, as what looked like an awry plot to attack the bastards was beginning to unfold. I may have even been instrumental in foiling that plot, but the screams that I heard as I fled were horrific. It sounded like a massacre, though I did not dare to look back!"

Perence Morden looked at the young fellow with an even mixture of doubt and trepidation for a few long moments. "I hope you're not pulling my leg, son? Tell me what happened, and don't skimp on any detail!"

"I don't rightly know exactly, sir. I fled as fast as my feet would take me," Marnard replied, "but I can tell you beyond doubt, both my mother and my father are dead by the hand of Jahl-Rin. I didn't see him kill my mother, though he told me in great detail how he had..." His throat swelled shut at the memory of Jahl-Rin narrating the gruesome act to him over and over, as tears began to well up in his eyes.

"Go on, boy." Morden pressed him.

"He...He r-raped my mother and tore her throat out after bashing her face into the ground until she died!" Marnard blurted out, as the knot in his throat suddenly released. "I walked into the barn by our house to see him over my father. He was cutting his throat with a large curved knife. I-I tried to stop him but he was just too strong. He knocked me out and when I came to, he was sitting there, eating my father's heart!"

Blaine Derwestle, Morden's chief deputy, brought his hand to his mouth and gagged. The stories of Jahl-Rin and his cannibalistic tendencies were legendary for hundreds of miles around. The terrible monster had now come to their town, and apparently turned it into a bloodbath. The rest of Morden's men stood at the edge of the large ferry, listening fervently to this tale of horror that passed from the young man's lips. They hoped these were just the ramblings of a lad who had too much to drink, and not truth. They started to holler and shout in a panic to Perence, to get on the boat and return home to see if this were indeed true. They all had families there; wives, children, brothers, sisters and parents. Perence himself had a daughter and son residing in Sarls Bend, and he quickly leapt from the pier to join the rest of his men, urging the previously oblivious ferryman to make great haste back across the bay.

"If I find this to be some sort of cruel joke, boy, I will have you drawn and quartered!" he yelled back at Marnard as the ferry took leave.

CHAPTER 8

Some hours and not enough miles had passed, as Joshua heard a faint sound approaching behind him along the road. He turned to see, with great relief, a horse drawn carriage not more than a mile off. Dropping his burden on the road beside him, Joshua waited in the hope of securing a ride to Terrinus. His feet ached, as did his back and shoulders. He was tired and sweaty. He shook his coin pouch as if to check he was indeed carrying coin. Of course he was. Joshua never went anywhere without a generous amount on his person. Still, it was a token shake, nonetheless. He would ask the driver what he would accept for the favour, rather than offer a price. Perhaps, and hopefully so, the driver would ask for naught. A free ride would be splendid indeed. Such was Joshua's way. Greedy to the end.

His anticipation became tarnished by the dreaded feeling once again of being watched. Whether it was that the driver approaching had merely spotted him, or who/whatever had seemed to be following his every move from Mills Wall to here, the feeling became more pronounced the closer the carriage drew. His chest tightened, and Joshua carefully sat himself down on the side of the road to wait.

* * *

Mellowood was silent as Scarlett carved a path

towards Joshua Melkerin. The forest itself made way for the tidy group of travellers led by Scarlett, navigated by the ravens, and coaxed on by The Sacred Blade of Profanity. Almost directly north, Astra Kirltth was at the true helm...at least on this plane. The Watcher oversaw the entire proceedings, including the apprehensive Joshua and his approaching ride. None but Astra were aware of The Watcher, who was the architect of every movement in the world of form involving Scarlett and The Blade. The sorceress had even successfully kept her own existence hidden from The Sacred Blade itself. This was a necessary stipulation of her involvement in the circle of participants. A broken, yet at once complete circle, held together by the intent of countless centuries of sorcery. The Watcher held the link securely to the sorcerers of old.

    Astra Kirltth was a direct descendant of the ancient lineage, and had been directed from birth by The Watcher, to carry out the necessary procedures to ensure the successful continuation of The Sacred Blade of Profanity. The Blade, though self-aware, was unaware of its own origin and oblivious of Astra and The Watcher. Here is where the circle was broken in one direction, yet firmly intact in the opposite. Scarlett and The Blade, of course, both perfectly aware of each other, were the primary players in this cycle of death. Each kill performed by them would fortify the link in time and space, to the moment of The Blade's inception, which allowed Scarlett to accomplish such feats that defied the physical laws of time and space, here in the world of form. The appearance of Huginn and Muninn fifty years past was a bonus of sorts, to aid Scarlett during a period of great turmoil, both in the world of form and in void.

    It had been the thirteenth time Scarlett had felt the sting of The Blade of Power, by failing to give it the required sustenance, which in turn had thrust her directly into void. Astra Kirltth had to go in after her, to extract her each time this had occurred, lest Scarlett be held there forever and herself become void. In such a catastrophic event, the thousands of years which had passed since the time of the ancient sorcerers of the Kirlt'th lineage would cease to be, in all time and all space, pertaining to those who had or were yet to have any contact, even indirectly, with The Sacred Blade of Profanity. The archaic seers had failed to *see* this disastrous pitfall when constructing The Blade Of Power and its originally intended purpose, and spent the rest of their inordinately long mortal lives searching for a solution that seemed not to exist.

The allure of immortality was profound, causing the sorcerers to make hasty and egocentric errors in judgement. At that time, nearly eight thousand years ago, the Kirlt'th faction were involved in a war of words with a rival faction of sorcerers; The Harrilluin. This had started merely as a slight disagreement, but the clash of egos led to a swift escalation, where the mere casting of words was inadequate. More drastic measures were required, and The Sacred Blade of Profanity went from being a thoughtform to a physical reality in the proverbial blink of an eye. This was extremely beneficial for The Kirlt'th sorcerers but before long, they were to realise that, maybe, more intensive planning should have taken place beforehand.

* * *

The streets were littered with the dead and dying; with agonised moans and cries of fear and despair carrying throughout the devastated Sarls Bend. Perence Morden and his men ran at full pace from the wharf, fearing the worst, but not quite prepared for what they were about to witness.

Morden's thoughts were fixed on his two children. His wife had passed during the birth of his daughter, the youngest now eight. Merryl Morden had almost herself died in the ordeal, but a heartbreaking choice had to be made in order to give the babe a chance at life. Perence loved his daughter dearly, and never for a moment held resentment towards her. He loved both of his children, but considered Merryl a gift from the gods. His son, Jaimen was considerably older at fifteen, and fiercely protective of his sister. He had grown up with the notion that Merryl was indeed a divine gift, and all three of them paid nightly homage to their departed mother and wife for her supreme sacrifice.

As they entered Sarls Bend, several of the men involuntarily fell to their knees in shock, mouths agape and staring in horrified disbelief at the scene before them. Perence very nearly joined them, but managed to stay composed and upright. The look on his face though, was no less mortified than his men, who slowly and shakily began to rise. Some of them started running towards the still living victims, while others could only stand, struck still in a daze. One of the rushing guards slipped on the disembowelment of a severely mutilated corpse, smashing the back of his head hard on the stony road, and joined the heavily injured in their wailing chorus.

The perpetrators of this unimaginable devastation were nowhere in sight. Jahl-Rin and his men had turned Sarls Bend inside out in search of Marnard before splitting into two groups to head in opposite directions, out of the town and into Sarls Bend's surrounding countryside. But not before sadistically murdering every man, woman, and child not fortunate enough to escape their wrath. That counted for most of the population of the small town. Perence struggled to maintain composure, as he stood in shock at the savagery he beheld. It was at that moment, the harrowing thought that his children may be among the dead broke his stillness, and he ran frantically for home.

His heart pounding out of his chest, the contents of his stomach pushing at the back of his throat, the dismayed lawman tore through the streets. He grew more and more distressed with each corpse he saw on his seemingly endless run. Thoughts and horrid visions stabbed and sliced through his mind without relent, and he felt he was running on the spot. The tears blinded Morden to the macabre scenery, whilst the pungent mix of ghastly odours made him heave, yet on he ran.

"Jaimen! No! NO!" The boy was inert. He lay by the foot of the stairs leading to the front door of the Morden residence. His right arm bent up awkwardly to cover his downturned head, and he lay, twisted atop his left. One foot rested on the bottom step. Morden's only boy was very dead. Leaping over the low fence surrounding his yard, Perence ran with a hasty stumble over to where his child lay, and fell to his knees in devastation. He carefully rolled Jaimen onto his back, and vomited uncontrollably all over his deceased son. The boy had no face. It looked like it had been eaten from his skull. Morden screamed through his regurgitations as he lifted Jaimen and ran up the stairs, through the open door into the house.

"Merryl! Dear gods, Merryl, please don't be dead. Please!" Perence gently laid Jaimen on the sofa, all the while hysterically screaming his daughter's name. He went from room to room in a blind panic. "Merryl! Daddy's home! Where are you? Merryl!"

The ground floor covered with no trace of his daughter, Morden bounded up the stairs, screaming Merryl's name incessantly. He searched every room upstairs, almost tearing doors from their hinges until he finally found her. The child lay curled up in the corner of her bedroom, hiding under a pile of blankets. She had been there for over two hours—she hadn't moved a muscle or uttered a sound since her brother had hidden her and urged her to be still and quiet. Jaimen had seen the approaching carnage and quickly ran to Merryl, who was playing out back on a swing. He had taken the surprised, confused child inside and up the stairs to hide her, then ran back down to do whatever he could to keep the marauders from finding his little sister. She had heard the yelling and the tormented scream of her brother, followed by loud crashing and smashing noises, as Jahl-Rin's men tore the place apart in their search for Marnard. Merryl was frozen in terror, and that was precisely how she remained—even at the familiar sight of her father, as he pulled the blankets from her and scooped her up into his strong, safe arms.

Perence slumped down on the bed with his petrified child stiff as a board in his hold and wept uncontrollably, blubbering inane half sentences that blended into each other, which scared the poor little girl even more. She still didn't know exactly what had happened, but it was obviously something horrendous. Merryl had never seen her father in such a state. The look on his face as he babbled transfixed her and made her tremble violently. She wished she could just disappear from this scene and wake up in a completely different place.

* * *

The carriage slowed to a halt at Joshua's hail, and he was greeted by a cheery fellow at the reins.

"How are we this fine day, sir?" the driver enquired.

"I am hot and exhausted, but otherwise greatly relieved at your appearance." Joshua replied in his most polite tone. "Would you be headed for Terrinus, by chance? I could surely use a ride in your fine carriage."

The driver gave a light-hearted chuckle. "Of course, my good man. If you don't mind riding in back with another. Otherwise, you are welcome to join me up here. I could surely use the company of your fine self." he responded with a cheeky grin. Joshua pondered for a brief moment. There was something a touch strange about the driver, but he considered the pleasure of Joshua's company would suffice as payment for the ride.

"I would be pleased to join you, my friend," Joshua said, as he picked up his bag and tossed it to the roof of the carriage before pulling himself up beside the driver.

"Then onwards to Terrinus!" declared the driver in an overly dramatic voice, and the carriage started once again along the road.

"Tummel's the name. I hope your journey so far hasn't been too unpleasant?" The man offered his hand in greeting.

"Joshua. Joshua Melkerin." he shook the driver's hand and managed a smile. "No, it has been quite uneventful. Just long and somewhat tedious. Thank you for stopping. My feet are not very happy with me at this moment."

Tummel laughed heartily at the notion of Joshua giving his feet a personality, and gave him a friendly pat on the knee. "Well, your feet can thank me when we reach Terrinus. It's always a pleasure to meet new folk in my travels. Alas, my passenger in back is not much for conversation. She is, in fact, dead."

Joshua felt the blood drain from his face at this statement, and Tummel once again laughed out loud at his surprised expression. "Oh, don't be alarmed, Joshua. I have been commissioned to return the corpse to her family in Sarls Bend. Heart attack, I believe."

"Oh." Joshua's relief must have shown, because Tummel broke into more laughter as he urged the two horses on with a good slap of the reins.

Joshua was slightly perturbed at the thought of travelling the remainder of his trip with a dead person. If he weren't so pressed for time, he would have considered staying behind in Terrinus to await the next ferry ride across the bay. As time would dictate, however, he couldn't afford the wait. His distraction back at home, and the prolonged attempt to calm his jitters, had caused him to leave Mills Wall much later than he had planned.

***

Joav squatted behind the large Ash tree and watched intently as the approaching group got closer. He counted eight men and recognised one to be Jahl-Rin. Among the remaining seven, he was relieved to see that Nerrik was not one of them. He kept still and waited for the rowdy mob to pass, then ran like the wind back towards Sarls Bend. He prayed to the gods as he ran that his brother was still alive and unharmed, but his inner voice taunted him with a very huge doubt. These people were savages, and although his brother was a competent fighter, he would not have stood a chance up against this lot.

He was only about a mile out of town and being so fleet of foot, he made it back to Sarls bend in just a few minutes. Joav slowed to a bewildered saunter at the sight of Morden's men, who were busy carrying the dead from off the road to the now abandoned Sarls Bend Inn. Those who had survived, albeit gravely injured, had already been taken to the town's infirmary. Joav stopped and looked around, not knowing which way to go. He couldn't see Nerrik anywhere, making him confused and overwhelmed. He just stood there, helpless and lost. Something told him his brother was gone. He felt it deep in his very soul, though he refused to believe it. Until he saw a corpse, Joav had to cling to the hope of seeing his dear brother again, alive and well, and reprimanding him for absconding without him.

"Joav! By the gods, you're alive! You had better come with me. I'm so sorry, but Nerrik has been killed." Marjorie Bregg ran to Joav and caught him just as his legs began to fail. She helped him walk a few steps, but Joav grew heavier by the moment, and she had no choice but to ease him to the ground. Marjorie had already watched her brother Arliss breathe his last as he died in her arms. Although she was beside herself with grief, she held Joav in a tight embrace. He was in a state of severe shock at the nightmarish scenario he found himself in. Nerrik was dead, and Joav could still hear the screams and wails of agony coming from the infirmary two whole blocks away. He bunched his hair up in his fists and began to rock back and forth, as his own wails of tormented grief gradually grew into screams of unfettered rage.

At the other end of town, the outside world ceased to exist beyond the walls of the Morden residence, as Perence held his dumbstruck and traumatised daughter. With time to gather his thoughts, he knew what awaited him downstairs and was loath to take Merryl down there. He could not let her see Jaimen the way he had left him; broken, faceless and covered in blood and vomit. He couldn't leave Merryl to go down and cover his son's corpse either. She still hadn't moved or made a sound, nor had she torn her frightened gaze from her father, or even become limp. She was frozen stiff, as though she suffered some kind of pre-death rigor mortis.

CHAPTER 9

Storm clouds gathered overhead, bringing a welcome chill to the air. Dera was more partial to the cold weather months, so this change lifted her spirits even more. The bread she had taken from the table at lunch would serve to keep her belly full easily past dinner. She had plans for the afternoon. Plans that may not see her home before sunfall.

The Prii did well to mask the solemn importance of today's exercise with a carefree, childlike frolic. They were well aware that The Sacred Blade of Profanity was on the move, and it would be a short matter of linear time before Dera Harke would be called upon to take up the Harrilluin gauntlet. The Mirror was more than just a portal for The Prii or a keepsake for Phenoluh. It was a powerful tool, created around the same time as The Sacred Blade of Profanity, with the sole purpose of keeping The Blade's Power in check. The Harrilluin sorcerers of old conjured and constructed The Mirror in defence and in response to the creation of The Sacred Blade of Profanity. Whosoever possessed The Mirror and learned its secrets, either unwittingly or with full realisation, was fated to carry on the now eight thousand year old war against The Blade of the Kirlt'th lineage. Although Dera was but a child of eleven years, practically her entire life had been spent in preparation for this war—a war that had no foreseeable end or apparent victor. Also, a war of which the young and innocent girl was oblivious. The Prii had made certain of this. It was best the child not know the horrors that lay ahead for her. That would only serve to drive her from her pre-ordained task.

It seemed unfair, but Dera Harke was The Mirror's chosen champion. Phenoluh didn't have the sensitivity of her daughter, although technically The Mirror belonged to her. Michael Harke may have served The Harrilluin well, but as fate would have it, his life was cut short through the machinations of The Blade and its warriors of Kirlt'th. Their Power had prevailed more consistently as The Sacred Blade Of Profanity had only once and only briefly, been lost and without a host to keep the Power in flow. The Mirror, on the other hand, had spent centuries at a time dormant and without a champion on several occasions throughout its existence. This inconsistency put the lineage of Harrilluin at a distinct disadvantage of Power. The only two factors working in their favour were The Prii, and the realm they had constructed to keep their order hidden. When The Mirror was forged, a veil was torn, which allowed these mysterious beings through into the world of form. The Harrilluin sorcerers had successfully kept this knowledge from The Kirlt'th throughout the ages. The Prii were powerful and elusive, yet their Power in the world of form was restricted and conditional to the proficiency of the one who bore The Mirror. Dera was extremely proficient, but lacked the centuries of experience held by Scarlett with The Sacred Blade of Profanity. Power does have an uncanny way of turning tables, however. Nothing can be certain in the realms of magik, and The Prii relied upon this uncertainty to realise their objective.

Into Mellowood, Dera and The Prii proceeded with playful haste. The trees illumined in magnificent colour, and the forest itself rejoiced in its own existence, as beast and bird joined with Dera and her friends unseen, in joyous frivolity. Dera felt lighter and happier than she could ever recall. She knew The Prii had something new and very special to show her. It was evident in the tones and tunes that permeated the atmosphere. On they travelled for some time, until everything suddenly fell black as pitch.

Dera stopped and remained perfectly still. The Prii, in fact the entire forest, seemed absent. The child stifled the fear that began to take her, and sat down on the ground she felt beneath her feet. As she lowered herself, Dera felt a coldness, as though she had fallen into the earth. Her descent continued, much to her surprise. She no longer felt the ground beneath her. Dera felt nothing but the chill of emptiness. Her first instinct was, of course, to resist the sensation of falling, but she rallied her courage as The Prii had taught her to do on many occasions. Dera let go of the fear and let go of her desire to remain safe and secure. At that instant—an instant that stretched for an eternity in the realm she had entered—Dera was neither here nor there, yet she was in all time and space at once. A fleeting moment caught in eternal Now, that catapulted her in every which direction, to find herself back in the brilliant glow of Mellowood Forest, though high amongst the limbs of the trees and certainly not where she had fallen into darkness.

The child observed a hooded woman; or what she assumed was a woman, judging by her garb and gait. With two ravens perched steadily, the trio moved seamlessly through the trees of Mellowood, which seemed to part and make way in a gesture Dera fancied being one of acquiescence or submission. At this notion, she instantaneously found herself back where this sequence began. Dera hadn't realised the silence until this point, as all the colours and sounds came flooding in on her in a split moment of confusing chaos, which settled back to normal almost as suddenly as it had commenced.

As soon as Dera had been jolted back to normality, The Prii enveloped her in a cocoon of vital energy to shield her physical body from the onslaught of her experience. Within this buffer, Dera *saw* the procedure through the face of The Mirror, and knew at once how this exercise in Power could be executed at will. It was as simple as allowing The Mirror's reflection to transform into the very darkness that had engulfed her, in which instance, Dera would be transferred to wherever she was intended to be at that given instant. Only whilst The Prii were present would she be able to perform this feat without harm to herself. This was a complex and dangerous undertaking that required a tremendous amount of Power, much more than Dera was capable of summoning and withstanding on her own.

As she slowly unwound from her heightened state of awareness, the darkness of night-time became evident. In what had seemed like mere moments, several hours had passed, and Dera was far from her home and mother. The Prii emphatically encouraged her decision to utilise The Mirror and the lesson learned, to bring her out of Mellowood and back to the cottage. No sooner had she gazed into the sheen of the glass, Dera was at once back home.

* * *

Joshua and Tummel arrived at Terrinus just in time. With a deafening crack of thunder, the storm announced its commencement with a sudden downpour, accompanied by streaks of lightning that seemed to tear apart the skies. Grabbing what they could from the roof of the carriage and leaping to the cobbled road, they made haste towards the nearest shelter. Joshua was drenched, as was Tummel, who laughed at their sodden appearance beneath the awning of the cottage where they took refuge. Joshua couldn't help but join him in his mirth. Tummel was an exceptionally jolly fellow, and his fine mood was beginning to rub off on Joshua. He was close now to his rendezvous, and this was purely thanks to the generosity of Tummel.

Uncharacteristically, Joshua felt he should recompense him for his troubles, and reached for his coin pouch. At the jangling sound of money, Tummel glanced across to Joshua.

"No, no. There is no need for payment, Joshua. We were coming to the same place, and I did enjoy your company. It had been a long, lonely trip with my silent passenger before I happened across you. I will have none of that."

Joshua reluctantly let the pouch go, and thanked Tummel for his charitable nature. He felt awkward, being in the presence of this man. He was more accustomed to the rude and blunt ways of folk he normally associated with, but Tummel seemed to be a fellow who didn't get bothered by much at all. A very amicable and happy go lucky chap indeed.

The rain began to ease, along with the light show in the sky, and the pair hurried across the road to arrange payment for the journey across the Bay of Solace.

"Allow me to pay your fare, my good friend. It is the least I could do to repay your kindness." Joshua offered.

"Thank you, Joshua. You are a real gentleman." Tummel replied. Joshua was taken aback somewhat. He had never been called a gentleman before. At least, not to his face.

Joshua wondered to himself if that was a yes or a no, but seeing as Tummel said nothing more on the matter, Joshua once again took out his coin pouch and handed over four silver coins to the ferryman. Together, the two men returned to the carriage to retrieve the rest of the cargo. The ferryman neglected to inform them of the incident across the bay in Sarls Bend —at least until he had secured payment, and had their cargo and luggage on board his boat.

When the ferryman recounted the events, Joshua sat slack-jawed at the tale of horror, but Tummel remained unruffled.

"Well, I guess I have one more for them to add to the pile." the smiling coachman responded, referring to the corpse he was to deliver. "I just hope there's some family left there to pay me for my service."

Both Joshua and the ferryman looked aghast at Tummel and his remark. Neither knew what to make of the strange man. His smile was innocent and generous. His statement carried not a hint of malice. Just very matter of fact and a little nonchalant. With that said, the ferry began its course across the Bay of Solace. Three men and a corpse.

Chapter 10

Across the bay, a head count of the survivors in Sarls Bend was underway. In Morden's absence, Derwestle had taken charge of gathering everyone in the foyer of the infirmary. The foyer was tiny, yet it easily housed those who remained and were relatively unharmed after the massacre. Inside the infirmary, sounds ranging from weak moans to horrible screams, with all manner of cacophony in between, played as a ceaseless reminder of the day's tragedy. In the foyer, sounds of a very different nature were prevalent. Voices clamoured to be heard. Voices that carried the grief of loss and the rage of unsatisfied vengeance jumbled together, and drowned out the vain attempts of Derwestle to maintain some sort of order. It was clear to the lawman that should Jahl-Rin and his murderous tribe return to Sarls Bend, they would not be met with cowering, frightened townsfolk. These people were psychotically furious and ready to kill—and they hadn't yet seen their town protector in his present state.

Perence Morden still sat, holding his rigid daughter. He trembled with seething rage at the injustice he had seen here; the senseless and horrific murder of his only son; the devastating trauma inflicted on his beloved little girl; the desecration of the entire town. Perence Morden would not rest until Jahl-Rin and every last one of his band of scum paid with their lives. After much time and no change in the girl's condition, Perence laid her on the bed and covered her with a blanket. He kissed his daughter softly on the forehead, and she instantly went out like a candle by an open window.

Jaimen needed to at least be covered over before Merryl saw what had happened to her brother. Perence didn't know if he would be capable of this, let alone even laying eyes on his deceased son again in such a mess. The vision in his mind's eye of Jaimen's fleshless face caused Perence to retch, and he covered his mouth for fear of spilling his guts onto the bedroom floor. Merryl lay perfectly still. Satisfied that his daughter was for the moment safe, he left the room and made his way shakily to the top of the staircase.

Jaimen's lifeless body lay peacefully where his father had left him, coming into view as Perence descended the stairs. He quickly looked back to make sure he wasn't being followed by Merryl, and then continued when he saw he was still alone. The lump in his throat threatened to choke him, and the sting in his eye made the stairs wobble before him, as he slowly approached his son...

* * *

The boat docked at Sarls Bend, and a very anxious Joshua disembarked with his indifferent travelling companion. The ferryman helped them to unload the morbid cargo before setting off back across the bay. The town seemed quiet from the waterfront, as Joshua and Tummel began to traverse the road into Sarls Bend. As they rounded the final bend before reaching the open main street, Joshua sighed with relief. The street was empty, and apart from a smashed window at the general store, no sign of the bloody massacre was immediately evident. Tummel, on the other hand, was not so relieved.

"I really do hope everybody is not dead. I didn't drag this damned corpse halfway around the world for naught!"

Joshua looked at him and started to say something, but realised he didn't actually have a response to Tummel's gloomy statement.

"Perhaps we should head to the inn. We may find answers there. A drink, at the very least." Tummel continued. Joshua simply nodded. He was astounded by the insensitivity of this man, and began wishing he was in the company of Jahl-Rin. He just wanted to secure the deal and be gone from this godsforsaken place. The further along the road they walked, the more the two men realised the devastation that had occurred here. Blood-stained large sections of road, and a pile of guts that spread over several feet gave Joshua a shiver of revulsion. Tummel, however, remained unperturbed. Joshua quickened his pace towards the inn. He badly needed that drink.

Upon entering Sarls Bend Inn, the pair found it littered with corpses and parts thereof, except for one man, sprawled out on the floor with a smashed face. He was moaning deliriously in a semi-conscious state amidst a mess of broken glass and blood. The bandits had left behind one of their comrades, forgotten in their sudden interruption and ensuing rampage through the town. He must have also been overlooked and mistaken as a victim of the massacre, as the room was filled with the dead. Tummel casually walked over to the abandoned bar and picked up a large jug of water. Joshua thought he was going to tend to the injured man, as he made his way over to him. Instead, the odd coachman dumped the contents on the downed man's face, which only managed to stir him slightly. The thug was heavily concussed and barely responsive, so Tummel merely shrugged and headed back to the bar.

"What will it be, Joshua? Whisky? Ale? 'tis my treat." He looked back at Joshua with that larrikin grin.

"Uh..." Melkerin looked around the inn and out the window before turning back to Tummel, who was now making himself quite at home behind the bar. "Whisky. Strong." he replied somewhat absently. He feared he had gotten here too late and missed Jahl-Rin, therefore missing out on this lucrative deal. A good stiff drink was needed to gather his thoughts and work out what he was now to do. He walked over to the bar, and Tummel handed him his whisky.

"It seems the town is devoid of the living. Whatever will you do with this corpse? It doesn't look as though you will be getting paid for your troubles." Joshua queried.

"Why, I'll leave her here, of course," Tummel replied stiffly. "Easy come, easy go. She is no longer my concern. I'm sorry, I never did ask you. How rude of me! What business did you have here in Sarls Bend, Joshua?"

"Oh, 'twas a business proposition, the details of which I was yet to discover. It looks like that has fallen through for me too."

The two men drank in silence for some moments until the doors swung open and in walked Perence Morden. His visage showed plainly that he was not pleased with the strangers helping themselves to the liquor so casually amidst such a tragic, macabre scene.

"Who are you and what are you doing in here?" demanded Morden.

Both men were startled at this sudden entrance; even the imperturbable Tummel almost dropped his glass.

"A delivery, sir. A corpse to be reunited with her family," Tummel replied in as formal a voice as his surprised self could muster.

"And I'm travelling with him," said Joshua as Morden turned his attention to him. Joshua Melkerin did not dare let slip the true nature of his visit to Sarls Bend, especially considering the most recent events. He wasn't lying to the lawman... just not telling the whole truth.

"Well, while you're standing where you should not be, make yourself useful and pour me one of those."

Morden once again addressed the coachman, and then turned to observe the moaning, semi-conscious thug across the room. "Ah, it seems they have forgotten one of their own! I will take care of you after this drink." he said, spitting on the floor in the thug's direction with disgust.

The smile returned to Tummel's face as he graciously obliged. Perence strode to the bar, took his drink with a curt nod, and downed the whisky in a single gulp.

"What do you know of a gang of thieving murderers, led by a swine named Jahl-Rin?" Perence asked the pair. "Have you seen them in your travels?"

"We came across from Terrinus by boat, sir. We saw no such gang," Tummel replied.

"And you? How about you?" he addressed Joshua.

"No. Nothing. Like my friend said. We haven't seen a thing."

Joshua felt very unconvincing in his response. His face felt hot, with nerves tingling in what he thought to be a dead give-away, but the lawman seemed to buy it.

"Well, finish your drinks and be on your way. There's nothing for you in Sarls Bend. A terrible tragedy has occurred here today. Most of the townsfolk are dead. The survivors, I can assure you, would not abide strangers at this time. My advice is, go back the way you came if you haven't chanced upon Jahl-Rin. That is one crowd you don't want to come across, believe me."

"But, my payment?" Tummel protested. "I have travelled nearly a week with this corpse in my carriage, and it will take longer than that for my carriage to be rid of the stench! I am tired and I am hungry, and I am now extremely out of pocket. What would you have me do? My horses need food back in Terrinus, and I was relying on this payment to return home."

"What is the name of the deceased? I can tell you if there is still family living here." Morden replied.

"Family name, Birchley." said Tummel.

"Gone." was Mordens short response. "What was your fee?" He asked, walking around the bar and opening the till.

"Twenty five pieces of silver was the agreed upon amount, good sir."

The lawman withdrew the coin from the till and handed it to Tummel, which he received gratefully and with his unnerving smile.

"Many thanks," Tummel said simply, and turned to leave the inn. Joshua stood awkwardly as his travelling companion departed. Tummel had got what he came for, but what of Joshua's recompense? He couldn't divulge the real reason for his presence in Sarls Bend to the unyielding lawman, yet he was hesitant to leave without securing the deal with Jahl-Rin. It seemed staying in Sarls Bend was not going to eventuate in the planned rendezvous. Jahl-Rin most likely would not be returning now. Joshua decided it was best he just say nothing and leave with Tummel. As he walked away, Morden swung himself over the bar and picked up an empty bottle as he made his way across to the delirious bandit. This scum was going to die, but Perence Morden would make very certain that he would die slowly. He would regret ever setting foot in Morden's town. First, he was going to get information. By the gods, this bastard would tell him everything before he finished with him.

* * *

Many hours had passed since the brutal massacre in Sarls Bend. Had Jahl-Rin taken a moment out of his psychopathic rampage to think a little more clearly, he may have sent some of his men directly to the docks, in which case, he surely would have Marnard back in his keep. As it was, however, he had instructed his men to split in two groups, and take a wide berth around the entirety of the Bay Of Solace to meet up again in Terrinus. As they had arrived at Sarls Bend from the south, Jahl-Rin had not given the notion that the quickest way north was across the bay by boat any heed. This oversight was to be much to Joshua's delight as he stepped onto the pier at Terrinus.

"Melkerin, you sly prick!" Jahl-Rin roared across the docks. "Hahaha, at least something turns in our favour." The menacing hulk lumbered over to the startled Joshua, who at once felt a flood of nervous relief. "Tell me, Melkerin. Have you seen a greasy little rat skulk by, lookin' like shit and stinkin' of rum?"

"No, I haven't, but I am quite relieved and actually surprised to see you, Jahl-Rin, my friend," said Joshua.

"I'm not your friend, Melkerin. We do have some business to discuss though. Not here. To the tavern, ay? I could do with a drink and I believe you're buyin'."

Joshua accompanied the haggard looking bunch to the Anchorage Arms.

"So, I take it you went to Sarls Bend," Jahl-Rin stated more than asked. "We won't be doin' business there for some time! Hahahaha!" The bandit chief nearly sent Joshua face down in the dirt with a clap on his shoulder.

"Hehe...Yes, I was there. A little too late, it would seem. Or perhaps, I should say, I came just at the right time. Judging by the aftermath of your visit there, I don't think I would have had the stomach for the goings on that took place. Your reputation is well-deserved, I must admit."

Jahl-Rin leered at Joshua without reply for a few seconds, while his men murmured and muttered in amused agreement.

"You silver-tongued bastard! Hahaha! Don't think buttering me up like that will get you a sweeter deal. What I have to propose will earn you plenty of coin. Don't you worry about that."

As they entered The Anchorage Arms, Jahl-Rin headed straight for the room out back of the tavern. "Get out," he spat. The few patrons sitting jumped to their feet, and obediently went out to the main bar. Six of his men followed them out to get themselves some refreshments after their arduous search for Marnard.

"Fetch me and Mr. Melkerin here some pitchers of ale," Jahl-Rin called after them. A chorus of "Yes, Boss" was the reply. Goatus and Kohass, who had seemingly put their differences aside, stood by the door to deter any intrusion, as Joshua and Jahl-Rin sat down to business.

"Children. I want four of 'em. No older than fifteen, no younger than five. I want 'em healthy and fit. We'll come through Mills Wall in a week and a day. Think you can manage that?" Jahl-Rin stared intently into Joshua's eyes, and slammed down a sizeable bag onto the table between them. The sweet sound of metal hitting wood through cloth brought an immediate response from the avaricious Joshua.

"Of course! Yes, of course! Four children. I will have them ready, fit and waiting for you when you come. Be at my house on the eighth day, under cover of night, and I shall hand them over to you."

"Hehe. I like you, Melkerin. You don't ask questions and there seems there's nothin' you won't do for a price," Jahl-Rin mused. "...but friends, we are not. As long as you got that straight. This meeting never took place."

"Of course," Joshua replied.

"Good. That's that then. Where's that ale? We need to seal this deal with a drink!" Just as Jahl-Rin spoke, one of his cronies entered the back room with two large pitchers of ale and placed them down respectfully in front of the two men.

"Bottoms up!" exclaimed Jahl-Rin and drained his pitcher in three huge gulps. Joshua followed suit as best he could, but had to stop half way through.

"Haha, Melkerin. Disappointing," the thug said

mockingly at Joshua's pitiful effort. "Now, fuck off. You got some kids to snatch. We'll seeya in eight days." He shoved the weighty bag of coins at Joshua with a dismissive wave of his hand. Without another word, Joshua picked up the bag and placed it in his own, then got up and left quickly.

As he left The Anchorage Arms, he saw Tummel jumping up into his carriage, ready to leave.

"Tummel, wait!" Joshua called. The coachman looked back with a grin, and waited for his traveling companion. "I must get back to Mills Wall as soon as is possible. Could you take me there? I will pay you handsomely."

Tummel didn't say anything, but his grin and the welcoming swing of his head for Joshua to join him up front was answer enough. Once again, Joshua climbed aboard the carriage, grateful both for the ride, and also that he was not asked to sit in back with the smell of Death for company. Once Joshua had secured his bag atop the carriage and settled in his seat beside the eccentric coachman, Tummel gave a slap of the reins and hollered "Onward to Mills Wall!" and they were on their way.

CHAPTER 11

Scarlett and her companions had left Mellowood, crossed the Three Mark Plains without incident, and were now travelling down the road to Terrinus. Huginn and Muninn had taken to flight as soon as they had cleared the forest, soaring high above Scarlett and The Sacred Blade of Profanity. They scoured the landscape for Joshua, and any who might stand in the way of their target.

"We have company, Scarlett," The Blade Of Power spoke. The ravens had spotted the carriage as it left Terrinus, far in the distance. A few miles down the road and to the left, a small group of bandits were also crossing the plains in their direction. Scarlett felt The Blade pulsing with anticipation. Its hunger grew rapidly and began to consume Scarlett with impatient gnaws at her psyche. Her excitement grew alongside that of The Sacred Blade of Profanity, and she quickened her pace considerably. She suppressed the anxiety that accompanied her excitement, trying to push aside the fear of once again losing control. The last kill seemed as though it had just occurred, although a month had past. The Sacred Blade was ravenous for the blood of the profane, and it pushed Scarlett into a fast run towards its impending prey. Their intended mark, Joshua Melkerin, was well on his way north towards them, and travelling at an urgent rate. The Blade of Power was going to get its fill with Joshua, but the bonus of several more was too enticing a treat to let pass.

"Come, Scarlett...Run!" The Blade urged. *"Don't*

disappoint me. I won't abide!"

The ravens descended to steer Scarlett off the road, in a line towards the approaching bandits as she took to the plains like an arrow loosed. One of the men saw something approach at lightning speed that appeared as a glimmer in the late afternoon sun. Before he could register what he thought he had seen, let alone alert his comrades, Scarlett was upon and amongst them. As each man fell, one after another beneath the assault of The Blade, Scarlett howled with a chilling fury that echoed across the empty plains for miles around. Her conflict was paramount in the terrible moments of slaughter, between the righteous bloodlust that coursed through Scarlett, and the will to keep it from consuming her. Not one of the bandits had the chance to either defend themselves or even barely to react; such was the swiftness and ferocity of the attack. The Sacred Blade revelled in blood and instantaneous terror as it guided Scarlett's deft hand through the flesh, organ and bone of these wretches, drinking deeply of sweet, sweet profanity.

Huginn and Muninn croaked and cawed emphatically as the blood craze within the crouching Scarlett slowly subsided. As she stood up amongst the dead, the sound of yells, coupled with the turning of wheels and clamouring of hooves on the road, passed swiftly, then began to diminish. Joshua Melkerin was one lucky fellow. Scarlett's deathly shrieks had gripped at Joshua's heart unforgivingly, causing him to faint and at the same time, alerting Tummel to the unbelievable sight, as they happened to pass at that very time. The coachman whipped his steeds into a frantic gallop and fled the horrid scene with all haste, leaving a drained and exhausted Scarlett to watch her mark helplessly as Joshua escaped The Blade once again.

Scarlett was furious. She could not forgive her weakness of will which allowed this damned Blade to once again take her away from their purpose. This cat and mouse debacle had begun to get way out of hand. Scarlett sat heavily on the ground amidst the mutilated corpses, and angrily plunged The Blade down into the earth with a frustrated growl. The Sacred Blade of Profanity cared not. Blood was sustenance, no matter the donor. It was sated, and now happily wallowed in its blood drunk state, which enraged Scarlett even more. She seriously considered getting up and walking away, to just leave this cursed thing in the ground where it was, and go. She knew this wasn't an option, of course. She was bound, and couldn't break that bond or she would be finished. Another howl escaped her throat. This one devoid of bloodlust, with despair in its place.

* * *

"Dera, you'll be the death of me, child!" Phenoluh often said this to young Dera, who was constantly running wild and giving her poor mother over to panic. Though she said it half in jest, these words would one day come back to haunt the child for years to follow.

"Where have you been? You had me worried sick! You know I don't like you roving the woods after dark. Are you hungry? There's stew on the hearth stone. You can help yourself."

Her mother liked to talk. Dera figured she spoke so much, as she was speaking for two. The thought made her giggle, and she skipped over to the large pot of steaming venison stew. The child was still in the energy embrace of The Prii as she sat down to eat. The grounding effect of the meat would do her well. The Prii began to detach themselves, yet they stayed close by her.

This most recent exercise had served to boost Dera's energy and Power dramatically, and she was certainly feeling the effects. Her appetite was voracious, and she returned to the stew pot twice more, much to the astonishment of Phenoluh.

"What have you been doing, Dera? Running this whole time?" Dera turned to her mother and nodded her head vigorously, her huge smile melting Phenoluh's heart. She couldn't remain angry with Dera. The child meant well. She just had vast amounts of energy to burn, and Phenoluh was not going to try to stifle that. A losing battle that would be indeed.

"Well, I don't know about you, but I'm off to bed. Don't stay up too late, child. Goodnight." Dera rose from her dinner to give her mother a kiss and tight hug before returning to her stew. The Prii rejoiced in this display of Love, and bathed both mother and child in a comforting blue light. Phenoluh felt the slight tingle on her flesh, but put it down to the loving touch between Dera and herself. Dera knew better and smiled into her bowl.

As soon as Phenoluh retired for the night, Dera produced The Mirror and began to gaze into the glass surface. She wanted so much to try what she had learned one more, no, two or even three more times, but The Prii would not allow it. The energy expenditure would be too great on the child, and even The Prii had their limitations. No, Dera would have to wait at least another full day before she would regain the necessary strength to perform.

She reluctantly settled for holding different expressions, whilst examining her features in minute detail. It was a simple exercise in focus and control The Prii had introduced her to when she was very young. She could hold a single expression without a flinch for over an hour, and would often practice this without the aid of The Mirror; sometimes even without being aware she was doing it. This was one reason the folk of Mills Wall deemed Dera Harke a strange child. She would sometimes sit or stand for ten or more minutes at a time, staring off into space until she would realise people were also staring—at her. After about an hour of this and three large servings of venison stew,

Dera was definitely grounded. With a long, drawn out yawn, she too decided to get some sleep as The Prii withdrew, satisfied their young apprentice had returned to normal.

* * *

Joshua awoke outside his home with Tummel nudging him gently. Once he had been sure they were a safe distance from the disturbing encounter along the road, Tummel had pulled to a halt, and checked to make sure his passenger hadn't passed away. Joshua's breathing was shallow but constant. His heartbeat feeble but there. Tummel's attempts to revive him proved futile, so he got to Mills Wall as quickly as was safely possible, and got directions to Joshua's house once through the town gate. By the time they had reached Mills Wall, Joshua was showing signs of improvement, though he still had not roused, so the coachman just took him home.

"Feeling rested, Joshua?" Tummel said kindly but with a touch of cheek. "You gave me a scare back there. I don't know what happened, but one minute we were in conversation, and the next you were not! Did you see that terrible sight back there by the road?"

"No," Joshua replied quietly. "My head is pounding. What happened?"

"I couldn't say for sure. You grabbed your chest, and then you were out. I thought for a moment, I would be transporting another heart attack victim home to his family. I'm just happy you are ok and, as you can see, home safe and sound." he said with a smile that denoted a hint of self-pride. "So you didn't see what happened? It was unearthly! Someone—or something—was tearing through a group of people like a blur! It happened so fast, they didn't even have time to scream, but they were torn to shreds quite brutally. I got us out of there fast as I could."

Joshua started to feel a bit more revived after the coachman's colourful tale, but his head throbbed violently, and his throat was dry as sand.

"Thank you, Tummel. It seems I owe you my life! Please take this," said Joshua, removing his coin pouch and handing it to Tummel. "My business venture wasn't a failure after all. The man at the docks in Terrinus was the man I was to meet with in Sarls Bend."

"Jahl-Rin," Tummel replied. "He was the one responsible for the tragic event at Sarls Bend. I know him…in passing. I chose to make myself scarce at Terrinus for a reason, but we won't go into that. Just as we won't go into what your business was with him."

"That sounds fine by me," Joshua said, and repeated his gesture with the pouch. "Suffice it to say, whatever my business was with him has paid off well for me. Please, take this. It's the least I can do for all your help."

"Thank you, Joshua. You are a real gentleman. Shall I help you inside?"

"No," Joshua replied. "I'll be fine. Thank you again. Perhaps we shall cross paths another time."

"Perhaps we will," Tummel said with a hearty laugh. "So long, Joshua."

"Farewell, Tummel."

Joshua watched, as the eccentric but very friendly coachman departed, then made his way inside. He desperately needed water, followed by a much welcomed night's sleep in his comfortable bed. This had turned out to be quite the adventure. The darker, dirtier work still lay ahead for Joshua Melkerin, however—but not tonight. He couldn't possibly begin to plot the unsavoury task set out for him in this state. Tomorrow, after a good night's rest, he would get to work and earn his ill-gotten bounty.

CHAPTER 12

The return home to her hut in Mellowood had been a laborious, drawn out journey that drained Scarlett of what little energy she had left. The frenzied attack by the road was more taxing than any she had executed in the past. Upon re-entering the forest, Huginn and Muninn slipped between worlds and vanished for the time being. Scarlett slowly made her way home with only the dreaded Blade for company. It taunted her as she walked, which aggravated her greatly. It was because of The Sacred Blade's greed and gluttony that, once again, Joshua Melkerin had managed to unwittingly evade them and win himself more time on this earth. The Sacred Blade Of Profanity didn't see it this way, however.

"*You're slipping, Scarlett!*" The Blade chided. "*Had you not fought me on this, we both could have had our way. My hunger was great, Scarlett. You know all too well not to deny me in such instances. Joshua Melkerin could have been amongst the dead along the road from Terrinus, but you faltered. Why do you think you have suffered such a loss of your Power, Scarlett? I could feel the conflict within you as we descended upon those fools on the plain. Had you simply given yourself over to our mutual need, things would have been very different. It is not wise to resist me, Scarlett. You should know this after our inordinate time together.*"

Scarlett didn't reply. She knew The Blade was right, but she was angry and she was tired. Scarlett wasn't willing to give The Sacred Blade Of Profanity any more satisfaction at her expense than it had already taken, so she trudged home the whole way in a brooding silence.

Upon entering the hut, Scarlett drew The Sacred Blade from its sheath, then forcefully and with utter contempt, flung it to the ground to stick fast into the floor. She fell onto her bed fully clothed, and slipped immediately into a deep slumber.

* * *

The next morning, Joshua woke with a terrible thirst, and the headache he'd taken to bed with him followed him into the next day with a pounding vengeance. He lay still for several minutes in the hope of abatement, but it was to no avail. The dehydration only intensified until Joshua was forced to leave the sanctuary of his sleeping chamber and quench his thirst.

As he reached the foot of the stairs and rounded the corner to his long narrow hall, Joshua stopped to gaze upon the portrait of Pellegrin Melkerin. His great grandfather had been an imposing figure in the town of Mills Wall when he was alive and Joshua was a young boy. Joshua recalled coming to this house with his parents to visit, from their home in the city of Eve. He used to hate coming here, as his great grandfather would constantly berate Joshua's father on raising such a pathetic excuse for a lad. He never, in his wildest dreams, imagined that he would someday leave the affluent and bustling city, to take up residence here in the quiet and slow paced countryside; let alone in the very house that he had despised so much in his youth.

When Pellegrin Melkerin died, the house went to his father. Despite what the cantankerous old bastard thought of Joshua's father, his grandfather had already passed and there was nobody left to hand it on to. Joshua had a loving but, in his eyes, fainthearted father, whom he manipulated selfishly since his early teenage years. He had practically stolen the house from under his father as the years advanced on poor old dad, and his mind grew feeble and dim. Joshua simply moved in and took over without a care to what his father thought or said in protest. After only several short months, Joshua grew tired of his father's whining, and suffocated him one night as he slept. He had buried him in the grounds behind the large house, and within a year, had established an exquisite food garden where his father's remains lay... and so began Joshua's passion for growing vegetables and fruits of all kinds.

Joshua kept the horrid portrait hanging in the hallway as a reminder of how weak and useless his father was. As much as he detested Pellegrin, Joshua agreed with his great grandfather on one thing. His father was a failure in every aspect of life, especially in the art of raising a child such as himself. Also, the portrait had been in place for so long nobody had ever thought to see what hid behind it—until Joshua that is. He had wanted to remove it some years ago, and had discovered the lever in the wall that revealed the secret downstairs room. This would be perfect as a prison for the four children he was to acquire.

He greedily downed several large glasses of water, and his thoughts turned to the conversation he'd had with Tummel the previous night. His heart began to race as he recalled the mention of the incident near the road. He felt it was somehow linked to what had seemed to be following him all that day, and he was fortunate to have Tummel to get him safely away and back to his home. He didn't want to think what may have happened had he been alone on that road.

His raging thirst finally quenched, Joshua shook off the troubled musings and set about the planning of his commissioned task. His mind was fogged from the tiresome day before and, as it was a brisk early morning outside, Joshua decided to take a leisurely stroll into the town centre in the hopes of spotting some suited targets for later abduction. He would have to wait for the cloak of nightfall to perform the deed itself, but he had the entire day to peruse and prepare. Leaving his house, Joshua knew what he was about to do was beyond forgivable, but a deal had been struck. Joshua Melkerin was a man of his sullied, despicable word.

He reached the town centre, and headed straight for the curio shop. He would often sit in the store in a comfortable chair by the window, whiling the days away, deeply immersed in one of the many books which he sold there. From this window, one had a perfect view of the square and busy marketplace. Joshua could sit in obscurity, and scope the area outside for his prospective victims. He knew where most everyone in town lived, and contemplated whom he thought would be easiest to make off with in the later hours of night time, as the unsuspecting folk went about their day outside.

He already had one in mind: a young boy by the name of Ander Pendlestone, who was well known to abscond from his home and that bastard father of his on many a night. He would be perhaps the most accessible child, as Joshua would not have to risk entering a home to snatch him. He had a good stock of ether in the hidden cellar at home, which he would use to render the children unconscious, greatly reducing the risk of being caught. If he were not supremely vigilant in his exploit, Joshua would most certainly lose his head for such a crime. It was, however, a risk he was willing to take. It was a risk he now simply *had* to take, as he had made a deal with none other than Jahl-Rin. Losing his head would be the least of his worries if he were to cross him, or fail to deliver.

He absentmindedly went to twist the massive ring he had pulled from his deceased father's finger; a habitual action he performed when deep in contemplation. He looked down to see that his finger was bare. Joshua's stomach lurched when he realised he had taken it off before entering Sarls Bend and placed it in his coin pouch. Jahl-Rin had remarked what an impressive piece of jewellery it was on several occasions, and was forever trying to convince Joshua to let him have it. The last few times they had rendezvoused, Joshua had hidden the ring and intimated that he had lost it.

Now he had accidentally given it away to the mysterious coachman, whom he was never likely to see again, or so he thought. Just as he had made this realisation, who would come cantering into town but Tummel himself! Joshua jumped out of his chair and ran immediately outside to hail his recently acquired comrade.

"Tummel, my friend! Over here!"

The coachman jumped down from his carriage with his usual beaming smile, and came straight over to Joshua, carrying something in his hand.

"Just the man I was looking for, Joshua," Tummel said with a laugh in his voice. "I don't know if it was your intention, but the coin you gave me was plenty enough. I believe this belongs to you." It was, thank the gods, Joshua's ring. He handed it to the grateful Joshua and said, "Come, my friend. Let me buy you a drink. I think you could use one after yesterday's little adventure. I'm glad to see you have made a full recovery."

"No, but thank you, Tummel. I rarely drink so early in the day. I have a lot of work to do. I appreciate you returning the ring though. I had just realised it was missing when you turned up. Thank you very much, friend," Joshua replied.

"Very well," Tummel smiled. "You are welcome, Joshua. Another time, then." As Tummel turned to leave, he stopped and without looking back added, "I was going to tell you just how I came to know your business associate. Perhaps I shall return a little later in the day and we can have that drink?"

A flood of possibilities washed over Joshua at this surprising revelation.

"Yes, Tummel. Please do. I would like very much to hear your story and perhaps, afterwards, I may share something with you."

The eccentric Tummel turned his head back to Joshua and smiled knowingly.

"I will see you later this eve, my friend." With that, he returned to his carriage and rode out of Mills Wall. Placing his dead father's ring back on his finger, Joshua returned to his vantage point inside the curio shop and continued to scour the marketplace for victims. A new plot formed in his mind, and he wondered what Tummel was to divulge when they would meet again. He wondered, and also hoped, Tummel could be trusted with what Joshua planned to reveal to him.

* * *

He had been sitting for half an hour when that young ratbag, Peter Menser, wandered into view. He was a cheeky brat, who liked to stand over children who were smaller and younger than himself. Joshua viewed the lad with disdain, as he swaggered through the market like he owned the place. He was only twelve, and already Joshua could see this kid was a bad apple. Mills Wall would be a better place without Peter Menser. That was Joshua's reasoning and justification anyway. *That's two*, he thought to himself. *Only two more and we're on our way, Joshua.*

Gilda Sween and Ellie Horace were neighbours, and had been friends since they were both four years old. Ellie and her parents had moved to Mills Wall five years earlier, much to the delight of the two girls, who hit it off straight away and formed a very strong friendship. Gilda, although the same age as Ellie, was mature beyond her young years, and Ellie looked up to her as a mentor. Ellie was an only child, and Gilda was the oldest of several children, which gave her a slight social advantage over Ellie. The girls were inseparable, and would often stay overnight at each other's houses. *Perhaps,* Joshua thought, *I could catch two little birds in the one net.*

Joshua rose achingly from his seat, stretched, then left the store to return home and get some more rest. He was excessively tired, and fancied he hadn't had quite enough sleep. He felt he had accomplished as much as he could for the time being. Four children—all healthy and within the age range set out in the contract. Joshua was content with his progress, and dubiously pleased about his appointment with Tummel later that day.

He hoped what Tummel had to tell him was conducive with what Joshua planned to propose to the strange fellow. From what he had seen so far with Tummel, the man seemed to have moved around similar circles as Joshua. His unruffled nature in the face of risky situations suggested to Joshua that Tummel had indeed been party to plenty of unscrupulous acts. Joshua couldn't afford to chance guessing his new friend's character, however. If the evening's meeting revealed him to be a little more on the respectable side of the fence, Joshua would have to keep his plans to himself. These were the contemplations on Joshua Melkerin's short walk home.

* * *

Scarlett had been deep in slumber throughout the night and late into the afternoon. All the while, The Sacred Blade Of Profanity stood in the floor; its recent satisfaction keeping it quiet and sedate. The sudden and raucous arrival of Huginn and Muninn roused them both with a start. Muninn landed atop the pummel of the fastly secured dagger, while Huginn perched with wings flapping wildly at the head of Scarlett's bed. She leapt from her prone position to a crouch at the foot of the bed, frantically grasping for The Blade that at any other time would have been with her.

"Dammit!" she exclaimed as she realised it was just the ravens, and relaxed at the end of her bed with a bemused chuckle. The Sacred Blade Of Profanity still stood indignantly beneath Muninn. Scarlett laughed again. This time with a bit more guffaw. She was still angry at The Blade, and she felt its unimpressed demeanour at how it had spent the night and most of the day. Scarlett had a good mind to leave it where it stood, but that all too familiar lung pain drove her from the bed and across the floor to grudgingly retrieve the cantankerous Blade Of Power.

"*Joshua Melkerin is at large, Scarlett. He is up to something despicable, Scarlett. Scarlett...are you listening to me? It seems we have work to do once again...*" The Blade spoke with an air of malice to her, whilst the ravens looked on with interest.

"You had your chance with Joshua yesterday." Scarlett retorted, "And you subsequently had your fill. Let him be damned and you along with him. I need rest." Without another word, she sheathed The Blade and returned to the comfort of her bed.

"*A little testy today, aren't we, Scarlett?*" The Sacred Blade provoked her. "*You know, I won't let you rest while our duties demand. I have had quite enough 'rest' with my nose in your floor, Scarlett. I now have ample zest and all the time in the world to remind you of our duty, Scarlett. Don't fight me, Scarlett. I will inevitably wear you down.*"

She absolutely despised the way The Sacred Blade Of Profanity used her name to such excess when addressing her, as though it demanded her undivided attention like a condescending schoolmarm. It irritated her even more at that time. She was really exhausted, and in no mood to be harassed by the unruly Blade.

"Do your worst," she said bluntly. "We are going nowhere today." There was something in Scarlett's voice as she turned over in her bed to face the wall that relayed to The Blade that Scarlett was not going to flinch. In a surprising show of acquiescence, The Sacred Blade Of Profanity allowed her this small victory, and remained silent as she drifted back to sleep. Huginn and Muninn left the two to their respite, and vanished without a sound.

CHAPTER 13

As darkness fell across Mills Wall, Joshua paced impatiently throughout his house. At the sound of the approaching carriage outside in the street, he rushed to the front door and opened it, even before Tummel pulled to a halt. He had been mulling over what to say to Tummel all afternoon, and he would have to contain himself until he had heard what the mysterious coachman had to say. Joshua felt he already knew, and was more than excited to put forth his proposal.

Tummel stepped down from his seat and looked up to Joshua with his infectious smile.

"Long time, no see, friend," he joked. Joshua laughed and waved him in.

"Yes, yes. It has been so many hours! I have missed you, Tummel haha! Please, do come in. I will fetch us some refreshments."

Tummel trotted up to the door like an excited child, his huge grin plastered all over his face. Once inside and the door closed behind them, he turned to Joshua.

"Joshua Melkerin, you old goat you," Tummel said slyly. "It took me near a day to realise. I have heard of you, Joshua. We move in the same circles, and I am surprised we haven't met a dozen times before!"

Joshua felt his heart rate increase at this unexpected news. *Where was this going?* He thought to himself.

"You want to know my connection to Jahl-Rin, I gather?" Tummel continued. Joshua simply nodded, lost for words. His eyes fixed on Tummel, as he fumbled beside him for the bottle of fine brandy on the table. "That scoundrel bastard cheated me out of five Hells of a lot of coin, so I decided to get my own back out of the skin of his little brother. I found him wandering the streets in the City of Eve, drunk out of his mind. I kindly offered him a ride in my carriage to wherever he wished to go, which he quite rudely accepted. Only, I didn't take him where he wanted to go. As soon as his drunken singing and insults from inside the carriage died down to a delirious murmur, then to silence, I immediately set off to the Sunflight Ranges. I know the winding, treacherous roads all through those ranges like the back of my hand. Shall I go on?"

Joshua looked away briefly to secure his hold on the bottle and pour two drinks before turning back to Tummel and handing him a glass. "Yes, please. Do continue."

"I know of a secluded cave that lies so deep within the ranges, you could holler and scream to your heart's content, and it would fall on deaf ears." Tummel's face grew darker, and his eyes narrowed as he spoke.

"I kept him there for days. I tortured the maggot slowly. Jahl-Rin had ruined me. I entrusted him with nearly all the money I had in this world, and he fucken stole every last coin of it. I knew his brother could tell me what very few could. Where does Jahl-Rin keep his hoard? Where does he actually refer to as 'Home'?

"I swear those bastards are a terribly stubborn breed. It took me nearly four days to tear all his hair from his scalp, a small portion at a time. It took me nearly four days to slice all the flesh from his left arm, and most from both his legs. The bastard didn't talk. Well, that's not entirely true. He did scream. He begged for mercy, but I showed him none. When that failed, he turned to rage against me.

"He thought that perhaps he could break me instead by revealing to me why my wife had simply one day vanished without so much as a goodbye. He was wrong. When he told me his big brother had killed her in cold blood, and shared her with several of his men as the main course in a morbid feast, I didn't break. Instead, I cut off his fleshless hand just above his wrist, and beat him around his head with it for hours, only stopping periodically to revive him each time he passed out. Still, he would not give up his brother's whereabouts.

"After nearly four days of relentless torture, I became impatient. With no food or water, and minimal sleep for all that time, his resilience was impressive, though at the same time unbelievably aggravating. My own supply of food had run out more than a day earlier, but I had a plentiful supply of water. With very little sleep myself; the mind began to get more...creative, if you will. I built a small fire beside him, and pulled his right arm across it, rolling a very large and heavy bit of rock onto his hand, crushing it and pinning his arm in place. As he screamed and as I laughed, we shared a meal together of his tender roasted arm. I just could not believe the loyalty this man showed for his brother. Granted, I had to forcefully send cooked parts of him past his bite and into his throat...but he ate himself nonetheless. I certainly ate my fill too, and dedicated each delicious bite to my beloved departed wife...I hope I am not shocking you too terribly, Joshua. You did want to know."

Joshua Melkerin cleared his throat and took a sip of brandy. He could not believe what he was hearing from this smiling, unassuming coachman.

"No. Yes. Well, uh...It wasn't the kind of story I was expecting to hear, but it does give me ease of mind to be able to tell you my business. I'm sorry if my reaction is a bit stark. I really didn't see you as the type, no offence."

"None taken, my friend." Tummel's smile returned at Joshua's response. "Allow me to get to my point then, for I am very curious as to your proposal."

"Go on..."

"I never did get the information I sought, and therefore never did see my money again. He was still alive when I left him—but left him, I did. He would still be there, I imagine. Rotting and stinking out that cave terribly. Jahl-Rin eventually caught wind of my horrible deed and has been pursuing me ever since. My horses and carriage aren't particularly inconspicuous, and I was lucky to have not been spotted back in Terrinus. Perhaps one day, I shall find him without his gang around him, and he can suffer the same or similar fate as his brother. I daresay you are now carrying some of the coin that was stolen from me, but that is not your fault, and I will not hold you accountable. There would be some small satisfaction in getting some of it back in payment though, for whatever it is you are about to propose. I am inclined to accept your proposal regardless, but please tell me your plan anyway. It's helpful to know what one is in for," He concluded with a wink and especially sinister grin.

"Well, ok..." Joshua began, "Jahl-Rin has requested four children, between the ages of five and fifteen. I have chosen the four, and must now retrieve them and bring them here, to be collected by Jahl-Rin and his men. My main concern is the time constraints. I plan to take them tonight- or no later than tomorrow night- but it must be done all in the one night. If I fail to secure all four in one swoop, the town will be on high alert thereafter, making the capture of the remaining children a very difficult task to undertake."

Tummel listened intently, knowing very well what was to come next.

"If you were willing to aid me with your fine carriage, this could be made entirely possible. You would be paid handsomely, as there is great and obvious risk involved. With your help and if we work efficiently, we could be done in no more than an hour. I would gladly part with thirty pieces of silver for this favour. What say you, Tummel?"

The coachman sipped his drink and looked deep in thought for some moments.

"I will help you, Joshua," he said. "Remember though, I told you my horses and carriage aren't exactly a stealthy mode of transport. We must consider the possibility of being seen, let alone heard. Sound travels greater at night, and surely the town guard would be patrolling."

"I have given that much thought, and there is a way to remain undetected," Joshua replied. "There is a suitable spot, central to all the houses I must visit, where you could wait for me. The fields behind the town centre will cushion the sounds of hoof and wheel, and there is not much reason for the town guard to frequent that part of Mills Wall. We should wait for the very early hours past midnight, to ensure nobody is about. I can bring the children, one by one, to your carriage. The risk would just be too great, as would the effort, for me to take them one at a time, all the way back here."

Tummel emptied his glass and held it out to Joshua for a refill. Joshua obliged him and awaited his response.

"We have a deal, my friend. It must be tomorrow night, as I have pressing matters to attend to tonight. I hope this is satisfactory with you?"

"Of course! Thank you, Tummel. Once again, you have proven to be a valuable friend. It is a shame we hadn't crossed paths long ago. We could work well together."

"I believe so," replied Tummel. "That still remains to be seen, however..," he added with a wink, then downed his brandy in a large gulp. Handing the glass to Joshua with a burning wince, his friendly smile returned. "Thank you for the drink, Joshua. Tomorrow night, then. I must take my leave now. I will arrive to pick you up at midnight."

"Very well. Travel safe, friend. I shall see you

tomorrow at midnight."

As Tummel left, Joshua could hardly contain his excitement. It was a very rare occasion that he was able to share his secrets with another. It was even more uncommon for Joshua Melkerin to have a 'partner in crime'. He was very pleased with himself at how quickly this plan was coming together. He went to the hallway, glared back at the portrait of Pellegrin Melkerin for a brief, disrespectful moment, before tilting it and releasing the cellar door. He went down the stairs to prepare the soon-to-be prison, by removing what little amount of belongings he had stored down there, and taking them out the back to his garden shed. The small box containing several bottles of ether, he left on the stand in the hallway.

* * *

Perence and the rest of his deputies were hard at work, acting as supplementary grave diggers in the cemetery that would afterwards be filled to capacity. The number of townsfolk slaughtered exceeded eighty, and the injured totalled thirty seven. Perence Morden had left his son at home rather than pile him in with the rest at the inn. There would be a mass funeral for the deceased, but Perence would lay Jaimen to rest behind his home and in private. Merryl had since become aware of the tragedy in Sarls Bend, as well as the death of her big brother, and Morden had taken her to stay with his elderly neighbours, the Klesters, while he oversaw the morose proceedings to follow. Jahl-Rin had also torn through their place in search of Marnard, but had left the old couple unharmed, though terrified. Two deputies were placed at each of the entries to Sarls Bend, with strict orders to come directly to Morden the moment there was any sign of the bandits' return.

There was a confusing mix of terrible emotions running through the town as the folk tried to pull themselves together. It hung heavily in the air, and weighed each and every one of them down with an unbearable sadness, fused with anger at their helplessness to turn back the hours that preceded. Sarls Bend had lost its spirit. Nobody spoke of either the massacre nor anything mundane. In silence, they worked into the night, to restore a semblance of normality and dignity to their devastated town.

* * *

Marnard dropped hastily behind a low hedge at the sound of Jahl-Rin's voice. He knew he shouldn't have stopped once reaching Terrinus, but he was still trying to decide from which direction to leave the small village. The decision was made for him then and there. He had no option but to continue north, though the thought of venturing beyond what he knew for the first time in his life was a daunting prospect. As the voices got nearer, he heard his name at least three times amongst other drunken banter he couldn't decipher. They were still looking for him, which ran his blood to ice as he lay in hiding. He didn't dare look up to see where the voices came from, but shifted slowly and silently until he was practically inside the hedge. He waited a full minute after the sound faded to nothing before jumping to his feet and running for his life out of Terrinus.

The way north was open and exposed, but Marnard tore across the Three Mark Plains as fast as his feet would carry him, hoping Jahl-Rin wouldn't catch sight of him and pursue. He still clutched what was left of his rum; though the effects of his Terrinus bound indulgence had worn off for the most part. He still hadn't eaten a bite for nearly two days, and the rum had left his gut sore and his mouth dry. If Marnard were to survive, he needed to find food soon, and most importantly, water. From what he could see for miles ahead, the chances of obtaining either were somewhere between slim and nil. After ten minutes at full pace, he began to falter. His legs became stiff and heavy, and his lungs felt they would burst. Marnard slowed to a walk as he looked around him desperately in every direction. There was nowhere he could take cover from either the elements, or from the eyes of his former captors. Only the sparsely distributed, small protrusions of shrubs offered partial cover. He picked out the largest one he could see close by and went straight to it. Dropping to the ground at its northerly aspect, Marnard lay flat on his back and tried to regain his composure.

With closed eyes, he reminisced. The peaceful life he had left behind was over. He missed his parents greatly, and tears began to push behind his lids and seep out, then down the sides of his face. The unfettered rage he had felt when seeing that monster hunched over his father began to return. He opened his eyes and sat up. Marnard Gray knew what he had to do. Apart from the fact that continuing north would inevitably lead to his demise from starvation and thirst, Marnard's parents must be avenged.

Although it was well into night, the moon was just past full and the clear, star filled sky lit up the plains, leaving him exposed to spying eyes. Marnard reasoned that it would indeed be safer to return to Terrinus and remain in the shadows. Perhaps he would be able to pilfer a meal from somewhere, as he was destitute and famished. He also needed a weapon of some description. If he was to get his desired revenge, Marnard would need to replenish his depleted energy first. He stared intently in the direction of the village, scouring the desolate plain for a glimpse of his pursuers. The landscape was empty, and Marnard braced himself to stand before making his way stealthily back to Terrinus.

CHAPTER 14

Scarlett leapt out of bed with a start. Something terrible had just happened, and she felt as though a vital part of her had been callously ripped out. The Sacred Blade remained silent and dormant in its sheath as Scarlett stood bewildered by her bed. At that same moment, many miles away, Astra Kirltth was also jolted awake. Something had ceased to exist in this world, which made Astra retch as she stumbled to her stone table. An image of one black wing swirling unbalanced and out of control dominated her inner vision, and Astra knew instantly what this meant.

Huginn and Muninn had appeared respectively in Terrinus and Mills Wall, in order to track the movements of both Jahl-Rin and Joshua Melkerin. Huginn watched from the rooftop of the Anchorage Arms, as Jahl-Rin and his men congregated outside in the street. Back in Mills Wall, Muninn swooped from the roof of Joshua's abode as Tummel left to return to his carriage. Circling slowly above the coachman, Muninn observed Joshua closing the door to his house. The raven hadn't realised Tummel had noticed it above him, and in an agonising moment, fell abruptly from the sky.

"Bah! A lone raven! A failed conspiracy! What a terrible omen!" The coachman had drawn and cast a small throwing knife with alarming precision, straight to the heart of Muninn. The bird was dead as it hit the road. Huginn was also immediately drawn into a vortex of blackness, and thrust into void. Tummel had just unwittingly earned himself a place on the shrouded death list of The Sacred Blade Of Profanity.

Scarlett was overcome with an inexplicable sadness and unbearable loss. The life seemed to be draining out of her, and she crawled back into bed, pulling the blankets around her like a chastised child. The next day would see her unable to get up, unable to do anything but drift in and out of tormented sleep and depleted, emotionally paralytic bouts of wakefulness, as The Blade remained in stasis by her side. The loss was significantly greater for The Sacred Blade, as Huginn and Muninn had accompanied it periodically for millennia. There was no comprehension, as this was a precedent for The Sacred Blade Of Profanity. It was entirely unfamiliar with the sense of loss. It could only remain with Scarlett in a depressing state of empathy, which jeopardised the duty of Blade and Host, and handed the advantage over to the Harrilluin lineage for the time being.

* * *

Astra reached out to The Blade via The Watcher through void, but to no avail. This was a potential catastrophe, but Astra was well equipped to deal with such crises. Scarlett had weathered the past three hundred years infinitely better than any who had come before, much to the contentment of the ancient sorceress. In centuries prior, the carriers of The Sacred Blade Of Profanity ranged from competent to completely inept. Scarlett had been a welcome respite for Astra Kirltth, with her innate expertise in her duty to the Kirlt'th lineage. Scarlett's procrastination however, in performing the necessary Ritual of Cleansing, was putting the entire structure at great risk. This was manifesting in various ways, such as this tragic loss of both Huginn and Muninn. Even though the greater bulk of her time carrying The Blade had been without the aid of the two ravens, Scarlett had evolved and learnt much faster over the last fifty years, than all the near three hundred put together. It was uncertain how this sudden loss would affect the future of Scarlett and The Blade, let alone the future of existence itself.

* * *

In the quiet of the humble cottage just outside Mills Wall, young Dera Harke awoke with a surge of energy, unlike anything she had experienced before. The Prii were present in astounding brilliance, and the elation that they exuded swirled around and through Dera like warm currents of watery air. She was outside the door in the cool night with mirror in hand before she even realised she had left her bed.

There was no time to lose, although she was unable to ascertain the reason for this sense of urgency. She did know what needed to be done, however. The stars above her reflected in the surface of The Mirror, churning into a singular mass of light as her gaze intensified, and then the black. The descent/ascent was, this time, more pronounced and terrifying, but Dera held fast to her courage, as she felt herself dematerialize and scatter throughout the entirety of Time and Space. At the point where she was sure she would lose control completely, Dera found herself once again in the midst of the high branches of Mellowood Forest. Below her was a strange looking dwelling, well concealed amongst gnarled and twisted trunks. She observed a crimson haze emanating from the hut that puzzled the young child.

"*Why am I being shown this?*" she spoke within, expecting her friends unseen to shed light on this obscurity. The Prii were absent, just as they had been when she saw the woman, commanding the trees in the forest on her initial endeavour through the true realm of The Prii.

Instead, Dera felt a falling upward sensation, and she was standing inside the red haze, almost on top of the sleeping form of the woman from the forest. The shock of this jolted Dera back into emptiness, and she found herself sitting up abruptly, once again in her bed.

The Prii gathered around her, but this time dispensed their energy cocoon in short, concentrated bursts. The child shivered uncontrollably, but not with cold. Her Power had just taken another leap in development which, to Dera, felt just like she was bursting right out of her skin. The Prii continued feeding her these blasts of energy for several minutes while she sat on her bed, unable to either get up or lie down. The intermittent blasts increased in frequency gradually over this span until the cocoon became a constant, once again shielding Dera from the incredible power that had been invoked, and her shivering eased. Dera got out of bed and headed straight for the pantry. She felt like she could eat every scrap of food in the cottage and then some. Her hunger seemed insatiable.

* * *

His stomach twisting and growling with starvation, Marnard watched from the shadows as Jahl-Rin and his men walked away from the tavern. It looked as though they were leaving Terrinus, much to the relief of the tired, hungry lad. The desire for revenge was beginning to lose its immediate appeal. All Marnard wanted at that time was something hot in his belly, but he had no coin. He would have to acquire a meal by stealth. Avenging the death of his parents would have to come at a later time... *but that time will come,* Marnard Gray swore to himself.

He stifled a yawn, realising it had been a long time since he had slept. Waves of exhaustion ebbed and flowed through him as this realisation threatened to drop him where he stood. He had to stay awake at least long enough to find food, for if he were to succumb to the urge to sleep, he would risk losing the cover of darkness he needed to find his bounty, undetected. There was also no guarantee that his captors may not still be lurking in the village, and he would be damned if he was going to be back in the clutches of Jahl-Rin.

He crept silently along the wall of the fishmonger's, towards The Anchorage Arms. The place sounded empty though he couldn't be sure, so Marnard stole across the way to the back of the establishment and searched for an open window, which he found almost straight away. Placing his rum on the ground and heaving himself up to the fairly high ledge, he slowly pulled himself into position to peek through the window. There were no voices inside, but he could hear movement in the adjoining room. For a moment, Marnard contemplated dropping and leaving the tavern to look elsewhere, however, his insane hunger forced him to hang there a few moments longer before carefully and silently swinging a leg up to the sill and climbing inside.

The shuffling in the next room fell to silence, and Marnard froze where he was, crouched behind some large barrels. The moon outside cast just enough light into the room for Marnard to notice that he had been fortunate enough to have dropped into the store room. He began to salivate at the smells of various meats, cheeses and vegetables invading his nostrils. Marnard couldn't believe his luck, but knew he mustn't rush to plunder this treasure trove of tasty delights. Silence and stealth were of the utmost importance, if he were to have his fill and escape in one piece. The people of Terrinus were a rough, no nonsense lot. If he were caught, Marnard would surely be beaten to within an inch of his life, and he most definitely didn't aspire to that outcome.

He found a sack filled with onions, which he very carefully emptied onto the floor behind the barrels, then proceeded to slowly lift the lid of the closest one to him. Reaching into the darkness inside, his hand fell upon something quite large and cold. He removed it with great stealth, and discovered an entire leg of smoked pork, which he immediately began to devour. Tearing a huge chunk off in his teeth, he stuffed the rest into the sack and slowly moved to the next barrel to repeat his pilfering, while making short work of his chunk of ham. The heavenly taste of pig brought tears to Marnard's eyes as he wolfed it down and plunged his hand into the second barrel, pulling out a handful of flour. He dropped it on the ground in mild disappointment and quietly continued his search. Within ten minutes, Marnard had filled the onion sack with the pork, along with a wheel of aged goat cheese, a cob loaf of bread, three sweet potatoes and five apples. Enough to feed him well for days.

    The shuffling in the next room started up again, and Marnard once more ducked behind the barrels and froze. Candlelight passed by the open door while he peered from between the barrels, and the shuffling of feet slowly faded, as the room once again fell to the dim moonlight. Marnard seized the opportunity to move to the window, and drop the sack onto the ground outside. Pigskin sacks filled with liquid hung from hooks on the wall by the window, so he helped himself to one, unsure of the contents, and hastily made his escape. By this time, all thoughts of sleep had fled from his mind, as the adrenaline of this perilous adventure coursed through him. Jumping to the ground, Marnard retrieved his sack of food, his half full bottle of rum and ran like lightning back towards the Three Mark Plains.

CHAPTER 15

Joshua searched calmly through the closet behind his living room for his large sacks. Large enough and strong enough to carry a child in, they would lend a small element of inconspicuousness, should he have the misfortune of being seen carrying them to Tummel's coach. It was still a few hours until Joshua's new partner in crime was to arrive, and he had slipped into the controlled, focused persona required for the task at hand. He slowly and with purpose, gathered his tools from various parts of the house, and then laid them out on the living room floor in an orderly manner to scrutinize his collection. Everything must follow plan to perfection. Joshua was very professional in his approach to work of the dubious variety. He would assume the role completely.

Finally, Joshua retrieved the small box of ether bottles that he'd brought up from the cellar, and placed them on the floor with the rest of his arsenal. He sat in a comfortable chair to once again analyse his required tools of trade, and await the arrival of Tummel.

* * *

"Ander, you get back here this instant!" The young boy bolted from his house, clearing the steps on his exit as his father hollered after him. "I'm sick of this happening every godsdamned night! Come back here! You can just go to bed. If we have to wait 'til morning again, I will strip the flesh off your arse, boy!"

Ander Pendlestone didn't turn back, but kept running for the safety of his favourite tree. The gigantic oak was a good hiding spot from the rage of his overbearing father. He just expected far too much from his family, and would take his constant disappointment out on whoever was closest. All too often, it was poor Ander who bore the brunt. Tonight, it was his older sister's turn. She had been washing dishes, and let too much water splash onto the floor, for which she received a sound and prolonged thrashing. Ander got up from the table and yelled, "Stop it!" His father stopped alright. He turned to his six year old son with the look of somebody about to come to blows with a mortal enemy.

"How dare you..." His father left his crying sister and started towards him, but Ander was out of the room and out the front of the house before the irate father made it to where Ander had stood.

He slid under the dilapidated fence, got up and kept running, as he always did, past the oak and into the darkness of the narrow laneway that led towards the town's main road. He didn't want his father knowing where he hid of a night, as the oak was visible from the house. The roots of the great tree were immense, and Ander was but a tiny lad who could hide himself easily amongst them. Normally, he would circle the block a few times, and return to the tree when he was sure his father had given up the chase. Tonight, he decided to take the scenic route.

The look his father had given him that night frightened him much more than usual. He was a horrible, sadistic man. Ander hated him with a fierce passion. His mother could do nothing to stop her husband when he flew into one of his many rages, lest she become the target of his abuse. Ander loved her dearly, but even at his tender age of six, he reasoned that his mother was simply stupid for allowing it to go on. He had implored her on many occasions to take him, his brothers, and his sister away from here. Find another town, far away, and live a happy life, free of the violence. He couldn't understand why they stayed.

As he walked down the deserted main street of Mills Wall, Ander kept looking back over his shoulder, and up each and every side street and lane. Quite often, he had settled among the roots of the oak, just in time to see his father returning to the house after a fruitless search for his wayward boy. He had been wandering around Mills Wall this time for a couple of hours. He didn't know where his father went on these searches, and he was now walking a different route to normal, so he remained extra vigilant. As a result, he was more than a little surprised to turn his head back to the fore, and nearly collide head on into a pair of huge black horses. They weren't there two seconds before, and he hadn't heard a sound. Ander stopped and looked up in awe at these imposing, magnificent beasts.

"A touch late for a young fellow to be walking these streets, I say. Are you lost, son?" Tummel stood behind him, flanking him with his horses and confusing the poor boy. He had just been looking and, like the horses, this man was definitely not there a moment ago. A chill ran through Ander as he struggled to speak. Both horses gave a unified snort which echoed loudly in the quiet street, making Ander jump. He didn't know which way to look. It was as if he were being addressed by both man and beasts at once.

"How about I take you home, wherever home may be, my young friend? Your parents must be worried sick. You can ride up front with me if you like."

It was then that Ander noticed the horses were in front of a large carriage. He nodded automatically to the strange man, and the beast on the left lowered its head and gave him a gentle nudge towards Tummel. Ander couldn't see his face beneath the large hat he wore, but his teeth shone in a wide smile from his shadowy visage with an enchanting friendliness. He felt he couldn't refuse the offer. More to the point, Ander felt he didn't *want* to refuse. There was the promise of something wonderful in the man's smile. Something wonderful, yet mysterious and unknown.

Tummel took a step towards the boy, and Ander saw two brilliant, piercing points of light where the eyes would be. He stood enthralled, as the dark man came to him like a dream apparition, and gently placed a cupped hand on his back, between the shoulder blades, turning him towards the carriage and in the process, taking the wind right out of him. Ander saw stars dancing before his vision and he felt strangely dizzy. He didn't even recall being lifted up onto the seat of the carriage and, even though he was still awake and somewhat conscious, Ander had no idea they were now moving along the empty street, and turning down a side lane in the opposite direction to his home. Midnight was nigh, and Tummel had just secured the first of four before even getting to Joshua. Tonight, success was all but assured, and Joshua Melkerin was about to be pleasantly surprised.

This time, Joshua didn't hear the clattering of hooves, or the wheels turning and bouncing along the cobbles. He was surprised right out of his seat at the knock on his door. As the door opened and Joshua stood, aghast, Tummel couldn't help but burst into laughter. The expression on Joshua's face was priceless.

"What the hells is this?" Joshua asked in bemused astonishment at Tummel's brazen presence with child in tow. Young Ander stood beside Tummel, looking straight ahead as though Joshua were not before him. "They must under no circumstances know where I live!"

"The boy knows nothing," Tummel chuckled. "I slipped him a little something. Look for yourself." The coachman waved a hand in front of the stupefied child's face to no reaction. "He's not here."

"Inside, quick!" Joshua exclaimed, as he ushered Tummel and the boy inside.

"What did you give him?" Joshua asked, as he closed and bolted the door behind them.

"Oh, it's a family secret, Joshua," Tummel replied. "I'm sorry, but I am not able to divulge. Suffice to say, the child is effectively catatonic. He will be none the wiser when he awakens. You need not worry."

Joshua dashed off into the living room, and returned with a small bottle and a rag.

"If you are unable to divulge, then I am unable to take any chances," he said as he poured ether on the rag, and held it over the child's mouth and nose until Ander went limp and fell to the floor in a small heap.

"Very well…Each to their own," Tummel retorted with a shrug, as Joshua stooped to pick up the unconscious boy.

"Wait for me in the living room. Help yourself to whatever you might like to drink. I will be with you shortly." With that, Joshua headed for the hallway, and Tummel walked into the living room.

"*Impressive,*" Tummel said to himself with more than a hint of sarcasm, as he perused Joshua's carefully laid out arsenal. Perhaps this would be done more quickly and efficiently if Joshua were to give Tummel the list of children and where they could be found, then stay home and await his return. His way was more favourable.

As Joshua entered the living room, Tummel turned to him and offered this new proposition.

"If you were willing to raise my fee from thirty to fifty pieces, I would be happy to deliver you three more, providing you tell me where I might find them. Nobody knows me here, and I have experience in matters such as this. You need not risk being seen by your fellow townsfolk. All you have to do is wait here. What say you, Joshua? Payment on delivery, of course."

Joshua had to think for some long moments. Fifty pieces of silver was almost a third of what Jahl-Rin had paid him. A sizeable encroachment on his bounty, indeed. Being exonerated of any involvement in the actual kidnappings was perhaps worth the extra twenty pieces of silver though.

"And if you are caught? Or in any other way fail to deliver? There is now a missing child and come morning, the chances of securing the other three after tonight will be very slim, if not impossible. Can you guarantee you will not fail? My very life could be at stake here. You say you know Jahl-Rin, so you would know I don't say this frivolously," Joshua asked.

"I will not fail, my friend. Rest assured." The tone of Tummel's voice left very little doubt to Joshua that he spoke the truth. Joshua relented.

"Very well. If you are willing to take this risk on my behalf, fifty pieces of silver will be yours upon delivery of three more children. Come, let me pour you a drink, and I shall give you names and their whereabouts."

Tummel smiled warmly and held his hand up in polite refusal. "None for me, thank you. I must have my wits about me for now. We can celebrate when I return."

"Okay then," Joshua replied. Grabbing his paper and ink, he quickly scrawled the names and addresses of Peter, Gilda, and Ellie then handed it to Tummel. "Be careful and by the hells, don't get caught!"

Tummel bowed deeply and rose up once again with a smile that brimmed with purpose and fierce intent. Joshua was momentarily stunned.

"Until I return then, my friend. I will take my leave now." Tummel turned and showed himself out, while Joshua stood confounded by this sudden turn of events. He listened hard but couldn't hear the coachman depart, just as he didn't hear him approach, even though he had seen the carriage out front upon greeting Tummel and the boy on arrival. Joshua pondered there was a lot more to the mysterious coachman than met the eye.

CHAPTER 16

Astra Kirltth sat in her cave entrance, and gazed out across the Sunflight Ranges. The countless peaks bathed in moonlight served as a powerful scrying tool for the sorceress, who utilised their Power often. Scarlett and The Sacred Blade Of Profanity had been inaccessible to Astra since the untimely disappearance of the ravens, and she was running out of ideas. Joshua Melkerin was proving to be a most difficult mark to eradicate, and this Tummel character left a bitter taste in her mouth. There was something about this man Astra couldn't pin down. He was dangerous, and an extreme threat to their purpose. She needed to find Scarlett and The Blade before things went terribly wrong.

It was a last resort, and an avenue she was vehemently opposed to taking, but she was at a complete loss where else to turn.

"*Dogsa,*" she whispered. Without any hesitation, Astra stood and immediately left the cave for Mellowood Forest. Dogsa Kirlt'th was Astra's mentor, antagoniser, and grandfather. He had walked this world since the inception of the Kirlt'th lineage, more than twelve thousand years into the illusive past. Dogsa was a master of the manipulation of Time and Space. He had ventured into aspects of void that even The Watcher had no knowledge of. Dogsa Kirlt'th was a cantankerous and impatient teacher, and was forever chastising his granddaughter at what he considered her ineptitude. Astra herself was close to five thousand years on this earth and, by Kirlt'th standards, a consummate sorceress of incredible knowledge and Power. Not in the eyes of her impossibly demanding grandfather, however.

She knew she would receive admonishment for her failure to locate The Blade and its Host, and she wasn't looking forward to it at all. It annoyed her to no end, the condescending way in which Dogsa would treat her. It was insulting and demeaning to Astra the way she would summon him, yet he would still make her come to him. He was intolerable, but he had taught her everything she knew, for which, she supposed, she should be grateful. The hundred or so years since she had last called on him however, had passed much too quickly for her liking.

As she walked, Astra caught herself complaining about her lot, and swiftly put a stop to it. Her grandfather had that effect on her. He made her feel like a five thousand year old child. She halted and stood for a moment with eyes closed, letting her every thought fall to her feet and seep into the earth. At the same time, she swung her arms up from her sides, and brought her hands together in a resounding clap that made the ground beneath and around her shake, dissipating the last remnants of emotion that left her for the dirt. With her eyes still closed, Astra took another step and opened them a split moment later, to find herself deep in Mellowood and face to face with Dogsa Kirlt'th.

"Grandfather," she said in greeting to him as she took his outstretched hand, and touched the Kirlt'th lineage ring to her third eye. He stood, looking down his crooked nose at Astra.

"Has the last century shown you nothing, child? What is the purpose of this summoning?"

Astra felt her face flush hot. "I am not a child, and believe me; I would have preferred to let another century pass without being referred to as one. What do you mean, what is the purpose? You mean, you don't know? I find that hard to believe."

"I see you still haven't learned to control your tongue. Of course I know why you called for me. You have lost your connection to The Sacred Blade Of Profanity. Do you know how this has happened, and why?"

Astra tried to remain unruffled by her grandfather's provocation in her reply.

"The messengers have been taken from this realm. One has been killed, and the other drawn into void. I have been unable to tap into The Sacred Blade Of Profanity since. Even The Watcher cannot show me, although I am certain The Watcher is fully mindful of its location."

"Yes," Dogsa said. "And what do you know of this Tummel character? Can you *see* what he is?"

"No," she replied bluntly.

"He is no average man. Tummel is Harrilluin." Astra looked into her grandfather's eyes in astonishment. The Harrilluin were masters of both illusion and elusion. Astra Kirltth had never encountered a Harrilluin sorcerer in all of her five thousand years. This was at once an exhilarating and terrifying revelation. Harrilluin... Here? Now?

The implications of this were potentially catastrophic. This lineage had remained elusive to The Kirlt'th throughout the entire eight thousand years, since The Blade and the successfully hidden Mirror had first clashed. The Mirror had passed from hand to hand throughout the ages, always a step ahead of The Sacred Blade Of Profanity. Its only shortcoming being that except for the times it lay hidden, dormant, and unwielded, it had always been carried by those who weren't actually of the Harrilluin lineage. It was always an unwitting mortal that gave The Mirror its essential obscurity from the Kirlt'th. Unfortunately, this left it in the charge of those who had no innate knowledge to use it to its full potential. Yet, not even the powerful and timeless Dogsa Kirlt'th was aware of the existence of The Mirror's otherworldly teachers, The Prii. Dera Harke was safe… for now.

"What must I do?" she asked.

"You must go back to your hovel, and fall into cessation. I will reinstate your connection with The Blade and Scarlett, and will expect not to hear from you again for at least another hundred years… *at least*," he added for good measure.

"That suits me just fine," Astra retorted disrespectfully, looking at the ground to hide the animosity in her face, but Dogsa Kirlt'th merely smiled and said nothing. He was hard on her, but for good reason. He was secretly proud of the many accomplishments his granddaughter had performed in the service of their lineage, but he would never give her the satisfaction of knowing this. Astra's proficiency was due to her constant need to prove herself to him. Even when inordinate spans of linear time passed between each meeting they had, Astra had been expertly conditioned to do everything to the absolute best of her ability. At that point however, she was being sent away with the proverbial tail between the legs. Reproved and rebuked by her infuriating mentor, Astra left without so much as a farewell, back to her cave to sit in profound silence, and anticipate her reconnection with The Sacred Blade Of Profanity.

* *

"It is time you learned some difficult truths. Get up." Scarlett rolled over in annoyance, as the voice dragged her from her restless sleep. Towering over her bed, she was momentarily stunned by the presence of Dogsa Kirlt'th gazing down at her.

"Maestro!" she exclaimed, as she struggled to get to her feet. Scarlett took his hand as he helped her to stand, and reverently touched his ring to her third eye. Looking up into his piercing eyes, Scarlett felt the misery of the past couple of days evaporate like the steam from a hot road, following a heavy rainfall. Regaining her composure, she smiled sadly at her mentor and spoke. "What truths you have to impart, I am sorely in need of. They could not be more difficult than the questions in my mind that elude explanation. Things are not right in my world, Maestro. I need your guidance."

    Dogsa gave her hand a light squeeze, and then released it. His aura exuded great authority and Power, and Scarlett was both humbled as well as reassured by his presence. Maybe things would return to what Scarlett perceived as normal in her world, now that The Maestro was here. Having the company of another after so many years of solitude was also a great boon to her psyche, and Scarlett began to relax by degrees.

    "You have lost your connection to The Source, young Scarlett. The time is drawing nigh for the Ritual Of Cleansing, but that is not why I have come." The very mention of the Ritual he referred to made Scarlett recoil. She was well aware of this necessity, but dreaded the idea of taking that step. Although more than a century had passed since last performed, and although Scarlett had since groomed her will and Power immensely, the memory of that traumatic occasion made her balk with distrust in her ability to endure. She had nearly died that time, as she had performed the Ritual alone. It was only for the immediate actions of Astra Kirltth, that she was able to recover from the attack. Scarlett had forfeited the battle of wills with The Sacred Blade Of Profanity, and had fallen victim to its insatiable bloodlust, thrusting her into void, where she may still have been to this day. Astra had gone into void, like she had hundreds of times in the past for Scarlett, and the ones who had come before in the service of Kirlt'th, to bring her back to the world of form and nurse her back to health.

"The messengers, the ones you refer to as Huginn and Muninn, have been taken from this realm. Muninn has been killed whilst watching your mark, Scarlett. As a result, Huginn is unable to revisit here, and has returned to void where it will remain. You fared quite well before they came to you, and in short time, you will again fare well now they are gone." Dogsa Kirlt'th gave Scarlett a few moments to absorb what he had told her.

"I felt they were a part of me, and I feel a part of me is missing," Scarlett lamented.

"They were, Scarlett... and it is. They served a valuable purpose, and that purpose has been fulfilled. Now you must complete yourself to continue. The Ritual Of Cleansing will give you that completion, provided you survive the ordeal. There is something else you must know. The messenger was killed by Harrilluin."

"Harrilluin?" Scarlett was puzzled. "Who is Harrilluin?"

"Harrilluin," Dogsa continued patiently, "is the family name of a lineage almost as ancient as our own. Mortal enemies for millennia now. The Sacred Blade Of Profanity was brought into manifestation to end their bloodline, but they were, and still are, a very devious and elusive order. Just as we had crafted The Blade, so did they craft something to defend themselves from its Power. Something that nobody of The Kirlt'th lineage has been able to discover, such is their skill of illusion and glamour. For a sorcerer of Harrilluin to make himself known at this time is a perplexing event. Nobody on this earth has encountered the Harrilluin for thousands of years. It is our understanding that they have found a niche in a realm unknown to us."

Scarlett listened intently, as Dogsa told her things she had not known in the three centuries she had carried The Sacred Blade. She felt somewhat betrayed and wondered if The Blade itself was privy to these secrets, also keeping Scarlett oblivious to her true purpose. She was indignant at the thought that she was being played, being used for an obscure agenda. She sat back on her bed in thought. Looking up at the immobile sorcerer before her, Scarlett felt numb. Dogsa simply stood and stared. Not moving a muscle. Not blinking his kind and wise eyes. He seemed like a statue, devoid of life, which made her uneasy.

"Why have I not been told any of this?" was all she could think to say in response to this earthshaking knowledge.

"My dear Scarlett, you are a single grain of sand in the hourglass of Kirlt'th. That you have survived this long, and served the Kirlt'th tradition with more aptitude than any in the history of The Sacred Blade Of Profanity, has surprised and endeared you to us all. However, knowledge comes at the right moment, when those who have the necessary Power to receive it and truly understand. That moment is now, Scarlett, and I tell you now because now is the time to act.

The Harrilluin sorcerer has sided himself with your mark, Joshua Melkerin. It is imperative that you give Joshua to The Sacred Blade Of Profanity at the earliest convenience possible, but you must be very wary of this sorcerer. We are unable to ascertain what he is capable of, nor even how long he has existed. He is an enigma whom you must take every precaution with. It is uncertain if he is aware of you, Scarlett, so you must recall all you have learned, and use that knowledge to remain undiscovered. We will be watching, as we always are. You are never truly alone, Scarlett."

As she looked down to the floor in contemplation, Scarlett felt a ripple of heat rush over her. She looked up to see Dogsa Kirlt'th was no longer there. A terrible fatigue took her, and Scarlett rolled back into her bed and promptly fell asleep. The Sacred Blade Of Profanity said not a word.

Chapter 17

Joshua heard nothing, but he felt Tummel at his door a moment before the quiet knock. As he made his way to the door, he considered the very brief absence of Tummel as a bad sign. He was expecting some outlandish explanation as to the coachman's failure, but was stunned to see him standing on the step with the three children obediently standing by his side. All had the same blank expression on their faces that Ander wore, and all followed unaided as Tummel entered Joshua's abode. As he did with Ander, Joshua took off without a word, and returned with the rag and ether, administering a measure to each child as they dropped to the floor out cold.

"Please, make yourself at home. I will take them from here. Thank you, friend," Joshua said, as he began with Peter Menser. Tummel merely smiled and nodded, but didn't speak. As Joshua came and went, carrying each child down into his cellar, Tummel sat himself down in Joshua's comfortable chair, and poured two glasses of brandy. He took in the sweet aroma of the liquor, but waited until Joshua returned before taking a drink as a token of politeness.

When he was sure all was well and the task complete, Joshua returned to the living room. Tummel rose from the chair, and gestured for Joshua to take his seat before handing him his glass.

"Thank you, Tummel, my friend. I really don't know what to say. You have come through for me in a way

I had not even hoped for. It seemed you had hardly been gone minutes!" Joshua glanced towards the large clock in the corner of the room at this statement and nearly dropped his glass. Tummel indeed had only been gone minutes. No more than fifteen, in fact.

"What...? *How*? How did you accomplish this in such short time? Did you have them already in your carriage, and merely waited outside until you grew bored? I didn't hear you leave, nor did I hear you return. I am grateful, yet befuddled, Tummel!"

"That, my dear Joshua, is also a family secret," Tummel said with a sly grin and a wink, then took a slow and deliberate mouthful of brandy. "I don't wish to appear rude, but..."

"Of course! Your pay. I'm sorry, you left me with no time to count out your coin." Joshua got up and left the room, then returned with a small chest. Sitting back in his chair and opening the chest on the table, Tummel poured them both another drink.

"...aand fifty," Joshua said, as he finished his count then paused for a moment. He felt obliged to keep going, which conflicted with his inherently greedy nature. The chest looked as though it had barely been taxed, though he had indeed counted fifty pieces, as Tummel could bear witness to. "I don't know how on earth you did it, but you have saved me from a lot of work and risk, for which I am eternally grateful."

Tummel took a sip of brandy and smiled again. "Perhaps 'how on earth' is not the appropriate term to use in your inquiry," he said obscurely. "Nevertheless, you have your children, I have my silver. We both win." With that, he downed the rest of his glass and began to stand up.

"Wait," Joshua stopped him. "I didn't finish. Neither in what I was saying, nor in my count. I want to pay you seventy pieces—a bonus for an exemplary service." He quickly dealt out another twenty coins to

Tummel's pile before the coachman had a chance to protest his generosity.

"Thank you, Joshua. You are too kind, my good friend. I think we shall have a prosperous association in future. I am pleased to have met you." He picked up the bottle and both glasses. "One for the road?"

"Yes, of course. Allow me." Joshua took the bottle and Tummel placed the glasses on the table between them, as Joshua poured two more drinks. "To your health, good sir!"

"And to many more successful exploits!" Tummel replied, and they both emptied their glasses in unison. "I really must go, Joshua. It has been a pleasure. I expect you will soon have four confused and frightened children to tend to," Tummel said with a nasty chuckle, and rose to depart.

"Yes, I believe so. Farewell, Tummel. You know where I live now. Don't be a stranger."

"Oh, we'll meet again. Goodbye, Joshua," said Tummel as he walked to the door. Then with a wave and a smile, Tummel was gone.

Joshua went into the hall, tilted the portrait, and released the cellar door. He descended the stairs part way, and peered down into the darkened room. The four children lay motionless on the hard stone floor. With a tired but thoroughly satisfied sigh, Joshua went back up, shut the door, and headed off to bed. The hard part was over... and it hadn't even been particularly difficult at all. Costly, yes, but he couldn't have asked for an easier task. As he lay in his bed, he counted the days until Jahl-Rin would come for the children. Was it five, or six? It seemed like a whole week had passed since the meeting in Terrinus, and Joshua's head was in a slight spin. Partly from the liquor, and partly from the relief of not having to risk his neck this night. He gave up trying to work it out, and slowly faded into slumber.

* * *

Astra watched through closed eyes, as Scarlett paced back and forth outside her hut. She had re-established her connection thanks to Dogsa, and was relieved to find Scarlett was at least active and seemingly attempting to formulate a course of action. She felt The Blade Of Power, and sensed an imbalance of sorts. Something had changed. Astra knew it was directly related to the absence of The Messengers, and indirectly concerning the impending Ritual Of Cleansing. She would oversee the rite from afar as had always been the case, though she could not, under any circumstances, intervene. If Scarlett should once again fall to The Blade, only then could she act to restore the balance. The Sacred Blade Of Profanity, she feared, would be much more determined this time around.

Scarlett was contemplating the words of Dogsa Kirlt'th as she paced beneath the waning moon. She had awoken with a new sense of purpose. Her intent was strong, but what she had learnt about this Harrilluin sorcerer had her on edge.

"It is imperative we leave for Mills Wall, Scarlett. Joshua's time has come. He cannot escape his fate, and I crave his profanity now more than ever before." The Blade spoke with a malice more sinister than usual. *"I am also eager to taste the blood of this Harrilluin murderer. The loss of the messengers has displeased and grieved me to no end. He will feel my vengeance as I sink through his very soul. We shall right what has been wronged, Scarlett. Mark my words."*

Scarlett didn't reply, despite agreeing wholeheartedly with The Sacred Blade. The death of Muninn was a terrible blow for both Scarlett and The Blade, and the Harrilluin scum would pay with his miserable life. The sunrise was only a few hours away, and Scarlett felt sufficiently rested, but she reasoned that to leave now would only mean several hours of lying in wait at Mills Wall until the next nightfall, and she was not willing to do battle with The Blade in its insistence to strike prematurely. No, she would return to her hut and meditate on the words of her mentor until she felt the time was right to leave.

* * *

Joshua was having an appalling night. He kept waking up, drenched in sweat and gripped with fear, at the nightmares that inundated his short rounds of sleep. Tummel would be at his side, only to vanish each time Joshua would turn his head. That smile... Those eyes... Tummel was a monster and Joshua was in his clutches. Thousands of ravens sat perched anywhere and everywhere a bird could possibly perch. All cawing and chattering at once as they watched Joshua with evil, beady glares. Each time Tummel would disappear was like a dagger thrusting frantically into his flesh, only to stop when he was back at Joshua's side. The children in his cellar were everywhere else he chanced to turn. Their blank, sightless eyes staring straight through him, like daggers of their own. When he would wake, it was no better. His room cast malevolent shadows, and he heard the fluttering of countless wings, which drove him to seek sleep once again in the hope of dreamless slumber...but it wouldn't abate.

Just before dawn and after waking several times, Joshua left the terrors of his bed, and went downstairs to fetch something to eat. He would not return to his room, but stay awake for the day. He was shaken severely by his night time horrors, and jumped at every sound, as he went around the house to light each room downstairs. Today was going to be a long day, and Joshua was going to get no rest.

The deed was done. He couldn't back out now, though he knew he was going to be plagued by guilt and even regret until Jahl-Rin came to take the kids off his hands.

* * *

Dera woke to the sound of birdsong and the smell of breakfast, as her mother prepared scrambled eggs and freshly baked bread.

"Good morning, sweetheart," Phenoluh said cheerfully. "Did we sleep well? I hope you are hungry. I think I may have made a little too much this morning. I don't know where my head is at today," she laughed.

Dera nodded as she gave her mother a tight hug, then went to sit at the table to wait for her meal. She was quite hungry. Dera fancied she could probably even eat Phenoluh's share, given the chance. As Phenoluh finished preparing, she brought the food to the table and sat down to eat. Dera started wolfing it down as soon as the plate hit the table.

"Goodness!" Phenoluh exclaimed. "Slow down child. You'll upset your belly!" By the time Phenoluh had swallowed her first mouthful, Dera was scraping up the last remnants from her plate. Dera jumped up from her chair to go and fetch The Mirror. She sat on the bed as Phenoluh continued to eat, and proceeded to go into her usual trance of staring into the glass. After breakfast, Phenoluh cleared the table, and prepared for the long day at the market.

"Do you think you could not go wandering all over town today, and try to stay within my sight, Dera?" She said as she got dressed. Dera nodded without looking away from The Mirror. Of course, Dera would not be able to stick to such a limited area as the marketplace for the entire day. She would go on her usual little adventures. Just her and her friends unseen. "Come on then. Get dressed, please. I don't want to have to rush."

Dera placed The Mirror on the bed and changed into her day clothes, then returned to her Mirror until Phenoluh declared it was time to leave.

As they arrived in Mills Wall, Phenoluh was pleased to see that the town was very busy that day. A lot of out of towners had come in for the trade. Sunday was the busiest day of the week in the Mills Wall market, and this Sunday was no exception. Dera loved Sundays in Mills Wall. She and The Prii could go anywhere in town they pleased, and Dera knew that once her mother had set up shop for the day, she was free until dusk.

Phenoluh knew her daughter would be scarce all day, and it was pointless to even ask her to stay close by. Nonetheless, each day, Phenoluh would request, Dera would nod yes, and then act no. Once again, Dera reasoned that her mother just liked to talk so their humble cottage wouldn't be prone to lengthy bouts of silence. Dera was perfectly capable of speaking, and had forgotten what had caused her to fall silent in the first place. She was late to begin learning to talk, and it was the untimely death of her father that stayed her tongue for so long, that she had made silence a habit. A habit she would from time to time break, but only when she was alone, or occasionally with The Prii, even though The Prii did not use speech to communicate.

As Phenoluh began preparing her stall, Dera waited until her attention was diverted, and shot off through the crowd. She was heading to the north end of town, where people were scarce, and her favourite tree in Mills Wall stood. The Prii had more to show her. Much, much more. Time was becoming of the essence, and young Dera Harke was closer to the next, more daunting, stage of her apprenticeship than she could ever imagine. A darkness gathered in the realm of The Prii, which threatened to spill through the veil, and turn Dera's world upside down forever.

* * *

The morning wore on, and Scarlett remained deep in meditation, ignoring the prods and pleas of The Sacred Blade Of Profanity to depart for Mills Wall. In her introspective state, she played out the task at hand. As with the previous journey to Mills Wall, Scarlett would arrive before nightfall, and allow The Sacred Blade to lead her to Joshua Melkerin. There, the battle would begin. So different from a random kill, the despatching of a mark involved the conflicting premeditation of both Scarlett and the voracious Blade Of Power. Since the death of Muninn and the disappearance of Huginn, Scarlett had not uttered a word to The Sacred Blade Of Profanity. Despite its goading and frequent attempts to engage, the battle of wills; the precursor to The Ritual Of Cleansing was underway.

The Blade had been very persistent all that morning, but Scarlett was able to effectively shut it out. Her visit from Dogsa Kirlt'th had strengthened her purpose and honed her intent, although it was to be only a temporary boost. Scarlett was still incomplete, and only The Ritual Of Cleansing would remedy that. The ancient sorcerer of Kirlt'th had simply given her the required means to carry out her mission, and reconnect Scarlett and The Blade with his granddaughter. All else was dependent on Scarlett's own inner Power and determination.

Something within Scarlett, and not by the will of The Sacred Blade, told her it was time. Opening her eyes, The Sacred Blade Of Profanity suddenly burst into excited jabber, as she rose to her feet.

"Yes! YES! Come, Scarlett! Joshua is waiting for us! We must not keep him in suspense! Oh, Scarlett, hurry!" The Blade was maddening in its unrelenting push, but Scarlett kept her composure as she prepared for the mission, still not taking its bait. Without speaking a word, she left the hut with the insufferable Blade at her side, and

headed for Mills Wall.

* * *

Joshua stared out the window into the bustling marketplace. The young lass he had recently hired had her hands full with a steady stream of curious customers, and Joshua was left free to ponder the meaning of his horrid nightmares. He was beginning to wonder if his chance meeting with the strange coachman had been as advantageous as he'd first thought. He began to wonder if it was indeed by chance that Tummel had been on the road to Terrinus, just as Joshua had finished hoping for a ride. Everything that had transpired since meeting Tummel had seemed to go off without a hitch, but something unnerved Joshua about the mysterious man. Besides his story regarding Jahl-Rin and the unfortunate brother, too many unanswered questions remained.

He felt himself beginning to fade as the day wore on, and he remained seated by the window of the curio store. Exhaustion brought on by last night's broken, tormented sleep, and the several days beforehand of travelling and conspiring, was taking its toll on Joshua. His head began to droop without his consent, and his eyes began to flicker and close. Joshua began to drift along the plane between awake and asleep, as the sounds of Mills Wall blurred into the pictorial silence of Joshua's troubled mind. His chin touched to his chest, and Joshua jolted awake. A fierce, frantically repetitive stabbing pain attacked deep into his ribcage, accompanied by the vision of a dagger, screaming his name as it advanced upon him, and the intense, burning eyes of a woman. A few of the customers standing near Joshua turned to look at him, as he jumped in his seat with a loud grunt. He instinctively put his hands over his chest to shield himself from the perceived attack, and looked around wildly before realising he had begun slipping back into the nightmare world of the previous night.

As the people in his store returned to their browsing, Joshua got out of his chair and decided to go outside. He was loath to fall asleep and revisit that hellish land of blades and birds and…Tummel. Once again, Joshua was being watched by unseen eyes, and he was filled with dread by the memory of this happening some days ago. Walking off the urge to sleep would be of no use he knew, as the ethereal eyes would follow him no matter where he tried to hide. Still, staying in the shop wasn't going to be any wiser. He left his store and ventured into the busy marketplace, in the hopes of blending into the crowd, and evading the unknown entity that followed his every move.

* * *

Scarlett had timed her departure well. The sun was already well into its decline as she neared Mills Wall, and darkness would take its place within the hour. Reaching the Southern Gate, she passed through, undetected by the town guard. At a pre-determined moment, a cart filled to capacity with large stones along the inside of the southern wall suddenly tipped, its wheel giving way under the enormous weight and spilling its load across the cobbled path, capturing the attention of the two sentries as Scarlett slipped through the gate, heading into town.

"*So near, Scarlett. I can already taste the blood! He waits for us in the marketplace, Scarlett. We mustn't delay!*" The excitement of The Sacred Blade Of Profanity was beginning to rub off on Scarlett and take hold. No matter how much she tried to switch off and remain focused, The Blade Of Power would simply not relent. Joshua had slipped through their fingers too many times now for Scarlett to abide. She was not going to let him escape this time. As much as she desired to reprimand The

Blade and cease its impatient coaxing, Scarlett held her tongue and kept her mind quiet as they began to enter the more crowded section of town. Today was an excellent day to be in Mills Wall for the purpose of remaining concealed. Even at the end of the day, the town was a busy hub of activity, and Scarlett easily blended with the townsfolk to remain obscured as she entered the market square.

The time was drawing closer by the moment, and Scarlett's heart pounded with anticipation, intensified by the swiftly rising bloodlust of The Sacred Blade Of Profanity as they moved slowly through the mass of people in search of their target.

"Joshua, Joshua... Where are you hiding, you worm? I can feel the blood in your despicable veins. I feel your fear... Your dread. You know you have little time left on this earth. We are coming for you, Joshua. We are your doom!" The demented taunting of The Sacred Blade was threatening to drive Scarlett to distraction, yet she held fast to her resolve as she clenched her fists tight, and slipped in and out amongst the oblivious townsfolk. Oblivious, to all but one.

Sergeant Noel Hartren stood vigilantly by the wall of the town barracks. His trained eye was cast around the marketplace to catch out any suspicious or untoward behaviour. Scarlett's struggle with The Blade had indeed driven her to distraction, and her movements had become somewhat stiff and mechanical, which aroused the suspicion of the town official. As Scarlett shifted out of Noel's line of vision, he left his post and cautiously made his way in her direction.

Scarlett was beginning to succumb to the bloodlust of The Sacred Blade. It wanted to leap from its sheath into her grip, and clear the path of unsuspecting townsfolk to get to their target. Scarlett remained in control, though only barely, unaware of the attention she had gained from Noel Hartren.

"*Joshua!*" The voice of The Blade Of Power blasted inside Scarlett's head as they spotted their quarry by a hat stall, causing her to jolt and then stop. Hartren had once again caught sight of her and stood, watching her with keen interest as she halted, opening and closing her hands as if preparing for something inauspicious. Scarlett knew she had to withstand the overwhelming compulsion to draw The Sacred Blade and rush at Joshua, to end his life and appease its ferocious appetite for blood.

"*Scarlett! What are you waiting for? Here he is! He is within our reach and at our mercy! We must show him none! Do it, Scarlett...Do it now!*"

Her arm began to cramp from the monumental effort to resist reaching for The Blade, until the pain nearly made her faint. She had to hold out for not much longer, as the market gradually started to wrap up. A few of the stalls were already closed, and more were beginning to follow suit. Soon, the market would be empty, the day would give way to night, and Joshua Melkerin would be on his way to wherever he planned to be...indeed, at their mercy.

Scarlett felt her will sapping as The Blade turned its attention to her old wound. Her lung felt like it was going to burst, and her head swam in agony. She watched Joshua with as much intent as she could muster as he stood by the stall, obviously distressed and trying on several hats. The more she resisted, the less clear her thoughts became. Scarlett was dangerously close to losing control. This simply could not happen with all these innocent and unaware people around them. Her arm began to spasm until she felt a loud snap in her mind. Just as Noel Hartren resumed his approach behind her, Scarlett yielded in her struggle. Her cramping arm subsided and relaxed as it moved up and inside her cloak...

EPILOGUE

Dera hadn't left her favourite tree all day. Not physically, anyway. To the observer, the young girl was simply in one of her all too familiar trances, as she sat still beneath the cool shade of the low drooping branches with Mirror in hand. Her inner world, on the other hand, was seething with energy, apportioned by The Prii to her delicate psyche. Dera was being conveyed through a multitude of realms, all of which would remain with her on a transcendent level for life. A fast-tracked cramming of arcane knowledge that the child soaked up with infinite ease.

After several hours, Dera found herself slowing to a near halt as The Prii steadily decreased their flow of energy until she was standing in a realm that resembled a vast, dimly lit sponge. The atmosphere was thick with an orange hue, and Dera found breathing both impossible and unnecessary. She could sense The Prii all around her, although she was unable to see them in this inanimate world. She felt her physical body, unmistakeably present there with her sentience, but was also completely aware of sitting beneath the tree in Mills Wall.

Before her, the thick, tangible atmosphere began to swirl and take the form of a person. Dera closed her eyes and found, in doing so, she could actually see much more vividly. It was a man who now stood before Dera, only several paces away. They both stood facing each other for an undetermined amount of time, studying each other. The man before her was Tummel.

* * *

Phenoluh was just beginning to pack up when the commotion started. Straight away, her first thought was, *What is that child up to now?* She looked over towards the headwear stall of Mr. Tilly to see Joshua Melkerin turning away from the stand, as hats rolled and fell in all directions. He didn't seem to register what he had just done. He seemed pre-occupied with something else. Following his gaze, Phenoluh caught a fleeting glimpse of Scarlett as she stared at the stunned Joshua, while the sergeant behind her spoke loudly to the back of her head. Phenoluh wasn't sure if she had blinked or been otherwise distracted, but, just like that, the woman was no longer there. Moments later, the screaming started, and the Mills Wall marketplace turned to chaos.

Phenoluh began to panic, as she was still unsure what had transpired, and Dera was yet to show her face. She hadn't seen her daughter all day, and struggled with the choice to try and find Dera, or remain where Dera could find her. Within moments, she was relieved to see the young girl appear out of the frantic crowd, looking very curious and a little worried. Upon seeing Phenoluh, a half smile broke out as she ran to her mother's side and held her tightly, surveying the marketplace with a look of apprehension on her anxious little face.

"Help me finish packing up, Dera," Phenoluh said. The death of the town official was now on the panicked tongues of many. "Let's get you home, sweetheart. It will be dark soon and it isn't safe here."

Together, they quickly gathered their unsold stock into the cart, and began the hour long journey home.

* * *

Jahl-Rin had substantially increased his list of tenacious enemies in the last few days, but that didn't bother him in the slightest. His reputation had preceded him for years, and his small army grew steadily. Sarls Bend was quite a good position to make his centre of operations. In time, he would return with the numbers and make Sarls Bend his own. He was still furious over the brazen escape of Marnard, and was determined to track him down and break him completely. Jahl-Rin was always up for a challenge, and this kid was going to be his pet project...Perhaps even his protégé. The bandit brute was not going to let this little fish get away. Time was short, however. He was soon to leave for Mills Wall, in the hope Joshua had come through with the agreed upon goods.

Jahl-Rin despised Joshua. Loathed his type with a passion. He hated sly, sneaky folk and Joshua fit that description like none he had ever met in his travels. He did, however, consistently succeed in his many endeavours set forth by Jahl-Rin. For now, he was valuable—but only until he failed him. It was yet to happen, but everybody slips up at one point, and Jahl-Rin would sometimes wonder what the fat, silver tongued bastard would taste like. His thoughts returned to Marnard, and he had made sure to put the feelers out for this lad. He had people scattered all through the land and word would spread fast. He could only hide for so long...

©Toneye Eyenot - autumn 2015

About The Author

Toneye Eyenot lurks in the Blue Mountains of New South Wales, Australia. In his spare time, he screams bloody murder in two extreme Metal bands, and plays bass in a Punk band. When he's not terrorising people with his music, the release of his Demons comes through the written word. With one published novella, being *The Scarlett Curse*; book one in this, The Sacred Blade Of Profanity series, as well as several short stories, flash fiction and poetry appearing in an ever-growing number of anthologies, Toneye Eyenot is a dark shadow, slowly growing in the world of Horror and Dark Fiction. Connect with Toneye and find his works in the below links:

Website
http://toneyeeyenot.weebly.com

Facebook
https://web.facebook.com/Toneye-Eyenot-Dark-Author-Musician-1128293857187537/

Twitter
@ToneyeEyenot

Amazon
http://www.amazon.com/-/e/B00NVVMHVA

Goodreads
https://www.goodreads.com/user/show/35697767-toneye-eyenot

Made in the USA
Charleston, SC
06 September 2016